THE CHAOS PROJECT

Nishant Kaushik is the bestselling author of *Watch Out! We are MBA*, *A Romance with Chaos* and *Conditions Apply*. He keeps a day job with Infosys Limited and currently lives in Australia. You can find him on Twitter @chaosparticle and can also write to him at nkaushik.23@gmail.com.

THE CHAOS PROJECT

NISHANT KAUSHIK

Published by
Rupa Publications India Pvt. Ltd 2017
7/16, Ansari Road, Daryaganj
New Delhi 110002

Sales Centres:

Allahabad Bengaluru Chennai
Hyderabad Jaipur Kathmandu
Kolkata Mumbai

Copyright © Nishant Kaushik 2017

This is a work of fiction. Names, characters, places and incidents are either the
product of the author's imagination or are used fictitiously
and any resemblance to any actual person, living or dead,
events or locales is entirely coincidental.

All rights reserved.
No part of this publication may be reproduced, transmitted,
or stored in a retrieval system, in any form or by any means,
electronic, mechanical, photocopying, recording or otherwise,
without the prior permission of the publisher.

ISBN: 978-81-291-4482-9

First impression 2017

10 9 8 7 6 5 4 3 2 1

The moral right of the author has been asserted.

Printed by Thomson Press India Ltd., Faridabad

This book is sold subject to the condition that it shall not,
by way of trade or otherwise, be lent, resold, hired out, or otherwise circulated,
without the publisher's prior consent, in any form of binding or cover other than
that in which it is published.

Contents

Please Block Your Calendar	5
So What's Your Big Idea?	8
Customer Delight	14
We Are the Frooti Boys	23
A Favour for A Eurail Pass	38
Maps Will Guide You Home	44
Hareshji Aa Gaye, Hareshji Aa Gaye	53
The Name Is Rao–Bhaleshwar Rao	61
Number One Or Two?	69
Pain Tings	86
Kapoor's Angel	93
Do My Calf Muscles Look Sexier Now?	98
Professional Colours	108
The R Word	118
French Window, Mumbai Air	129
Santro	135
You Deserve a Discount	143
Inner Peace	150

Baba Bhai	163
Hair We Are	179
Rating: Not Applicable	191
Party on My Mind	197
Big Teachers Don't Cry	211
Fall From Grace	218
The Resurgence	226
The End of the Beginning	235

I feel on top of the world. Copies of my dream novel are stacked in a spiral at the entrance of the bookstore. A young boy, who I am going to start hating in about a hundred seconds, looks at the spiral in awe. He picks up a copy, reads the synopsis, wails so shrilly he almost shatters his mother's reading glasses. Then he angrily flings the copy like a frisbee and narrowly misses knocking the emcee of the event down. Seconds later, the beautiful spiral, so elegantly built with copies of my labour of love, comes crashing down and becomes a debris-pile the way my dreams have so often in the year gone by.

'I don't want shitty books, I want Superman,' he wails. His mother looks at the staff, half-confused, half-apologetic. I walk up to the boy and ruffle his hair lovingly. In my mind, of course, I yank the hair off his head rather violently. But given that I am suited up for an important occasion, I downplay my inner feelings and buy him a cheap Superman toy from the shelf. His mother starts the customary 'Oh, this was not necessary' drama. I give her the uncustomary 'Read between the lines, lady!' look. She looks at the debris of books being reassembled by the staff, reluctantly picks up a copy, pays up and drags her jubilant boy out of the store.

Meanwhile, the grand total of three journalists with cameramen who have turned up to cover my event, are now getting crabby. They want to leave, the chief guest is nowhere in sight yet, and neither are the snacks that had been promised in the press invite. I plead with them to wait. Ok, but only for half an hour they declare, as though their newspapers will shut down in their absence.

Apparently, Mallika Sherawat is returning to India and they need to go cover her (not literally, one of them says and laughs alone). I hint at the possibility that I also may have called someone worth covering, and they start prodding me to disclose the name of the chief guest. I try to avoid the discussion, but the over enthusiastic emcee comes beaming before them and screams like a mad fan girl, 'DINO MOREA!' Whatever little patience the journalists had left, now quite properly disappears. They are upset with me for sending an exaggerated press note that mentioned 'surprise celebrity and media magnet will preside…'

This is so annoying. I spend the next ten minutes explaining myself to them: How I had initially approached Shahrukh Khan's office and his receptionist had said, 'Sir would charge twenty-five lakhs for the appearance.' I explained he only had to come snip a ribbon off the book, I was not asking him to purchase the bookstore. Unfortunately the deal didn't work out because the receptionist started behaving like she was Shahrukh herself. Someone told me to approach Dino Morea instead, because he was very humble and mostly very free also. His business manager confirmed that Dino would surely come, in fact he might bring along some like-minded friends from the industry for added media pull.

Having reeled off my saga I look at them expectantly and am not disappointed. After some bickering, we come to an agreement: the photographers will quickly do a small photo-op with me and then leave for the airport to take pictures of Mallika Sherawat. The scribes stay back because they concede they have the same questions to ask her that they did two years ago, and agree they can dig them out from the archives.

People have started pouring in. Some have taken their seats in front of the podium and are getting a little restless. Mehek suggests I begin the event without Dino Morea. I am about to start howling my lungs out [this section in itals is replicated from around pg 131 onward, and there the author uses the highlighted words], when Dino's business manager calls my cell and tells me to come to the gate. I rush out excitedly; a sedan pulls over and a fat, bald, middle-aged, sweaty man walks out and waves at me. The sedan drives away. Frankly, I have never seen a Dino Morea movie but I don't think this is what he looks like. Mehek confirms my suspicion. The bald man comes and introduces himself as Dino Morea's business manager.

'Sir has got into a very tight gym regime for his new look in a superhero film,' the business manager explains, 'so he is very tired. He has sent me to cut your ribbon instead.'

Soon I have tears in my eyes, not so much because of Dino's no-show as by this egghead trying to hog the limelight at the event. He was supposed to launch my book, then shut up and sit in a corner and let me read paragraphs from my book. Instead, he starts drawing parallels between Dino's early struggle and my early reckoning in the field of literature. If I had abs like a hero's, I wouldn't be sobbing about 'struggles'. At least thrice he mentions I will need to work very hard to be successful like Dino Morea. I am about to slap him now. Thankfully, he concludes his speech by handing me a rolled-up sheet decorated with a pink ribbon.

'A memo from Dino Sir,' he announces as I unravel the sheet.

It turns out to be a poster of Dino Morea wearing nothing but leather pants, and a message below, 'To the author it may concern:

Love, luck and XOXO – Dino.'

By now I have lost context of what this event was all about. The emcee reminds me, and so prompted I read out my selected selections. Customary applause. Staccato yawns escape pursed mouths. From the crowd, an odd whisper: 'Every-bloody-body is becoming an author now.' I am about to throw the microphone in the direction of that voice, but am held back by a sudden question that winds me back to when it all started.

'What prompted you to be a writer?'

1

Please Block Your Calendar

MEHEK INSISTS IT has to do with how her love and encouragement drove me to pursue my dream. Last month during our Phuket holiday (horrible trip; I botched up my research, confusing Pattaya with Phuket) she reminded me for the third time it was she who had convinced me to participate in the international essay symposium—the place where it all started. I kept quiet the first two times, but the third time I countered her claim; it was my father who had actually told me about the symposium. Silence engulfed the sea beach where we lay wasted. Then, the sound of heavy breathing. A ferocious wave welled up in Mehek's eyes as I asked her what was wrong, to which she obviously said 'Nothing!' After which she obviously mentioned that I had no value for her contribution to my success and I anyway never cared about her aspirations the way she did about mine and why didn't I date my father instead.

Our Phuket trip was cut short by a day. I could have

considered this an upside of our bitter argument, only the useless, weirdly-accented airport authorities messed up our luggage transportation and got us to collect it in transit from Kuala Lumpur despite knowing we didn't have a Malaysian visa.

We were detained at the Kuala Lumpur airport for over six hours and cross-examined for God knows what. Unnecessarily hyper. Have you seen the public toilets in Kuala Lumpur? Their commodes have instructions written on them: 'Please do not stand on the toilet seat.' Can someone explain this paranoia to me? Why would someone aim his poo at a commode from three feet above? Why would two innocent travellers, one of whom is a reputed novelist at the national level, bother to discreetly enter your country? If we have to plunder your wealth, Kuala Lumpur, we would rather go to Chennai. But no. The officers expended their share of sadism before putting us on the next flight to Mumbai. By the time we got home, Mehek had reminded me about thirty times that I should not try speaking to her until further notice.

She can be so cute, five out of ten times. Well, she thought her silent treatment was going to kill me.

What does she know...of how much I love her. Mehek defines my very existence. Maybe some day she will realize that being angry with me is totally futile because I was only meant to bring joy to her life. I love her. I am what I am today because...

...Sorry for that brief interruption. I was typing away and suddenly realized she was peering over my shoulder on the pretext of looking for her reading glasses. She has become very suspicious of me lately.

For example, the time I accidentally bumped into Bipasha

Basu at The Marriott and gave her a copy of my book without charging her for it. 'What is so special about Bipasha that she should get a free copy of your book?' and all that. God. I think it is this ridiculously stressful job she has taken on at Goldman Sachs. She was once so full of life. There was a time she used to so easily slip into my arms. These days, she will only 'revert at the soonest after checking my calendar'.

This entire month, confined to forced solitude in my study where I am typing right now, I got an opportunity to start on my success story—from an envied fast-tracker at one of the country's largest consulting giants to a writing prodigy who recently featured #38 in 'Rising Youth In Indian Literature' by *Jansatta*.

This story is about me, the man who grew up watching preachy films that counsel you to follow your dream without fear, and none of which talk about what terrible things happen after you start following your dream. This story spotlights those terrible things. Sit back, relax, get inspired if you want to but don't try any of this stuff yourself unless you have an appetite for misadventure.

2

So What's Your Big Idea?

INSPIRATION HITS YOU at the most unlikely times and in various forms. Some famous people claim they began chasing their dreams from the time they wore their first nappy. I shan't peddle any such rubbish here. To be honest I had failed to recognize my inner potential until a random blog (that I had started writing only to vent my frustration at the alarming levels of mediocrity and stupidity I suffered all around me at work), caught the fancy of a certain Brian Jones from Crown, a literary agency somewhere in the United States.

'Your prose is sharp, engaging and assertive,' his email said, and that he was glad to learn that I had, 'also been shortlisted as one of the finalists at the Young Turks Literary Symposium in Switzerland'. When he requested a telephonic appointment to discuss 'an interesting business opportunity', I initially dismissed the request as just one of the many soliciting mails I had been getting from the fan subscribers of my blog. When he insisted,

I told him I would check my calendar and look up a free slot that week, if there would be one at all.

Between you and me, I was hardly busy. Four months had passed since I had once again seen Bytesphere through a successful telecom consulting deal in Singapore, and had regrettably turned down the offer to get poached by the client. Idling away my time at the workplace had felt like good fun, but only until Mehek put in her papers and sought greener pastures at Goldman Sachs with an investment banking role. Besides the fact that I would sorely miss her presence at work, I was also severely nauseated when she told me what salary Goldman Sachs was offering her. I suddenly started hating Bytesphere—the sound of the very name; the sight of that ugly, ominous building; the smell of my desk, from which I had just thrown out three-week old empty boxes of chicken rolls ordered from Faasos.

I admit I had come to command a lot of respect in the company. I had risen through the ranks at breakneck speed and driven my contemporaries red with envy. But then it was not like the company had done me a favour. This was the least that I could expect as the employee who had almost single-handedly helped Bytesphere retain a dying relationship with an Australian client, subsequently making it a fat cash cow that could be milked forever; the employee who had shot the organization to fame with that goodwill project in rural India; the employee who may have accidentally sold Bytesphere's proprietary software testing tool to Modern Bank of Vietnam but had later calmly recovered it by way of certain covert and confidential compromises.

Also, while I had acquired the kind of stature that could let me throw some weight around, I continued to be nice to the company. Even when Anand our unit head created a specially designed role for me as 'Advisory Contact for New Employees', better known as ACNE, so I could mentor and train new recruits under my leadership, I embraced the challenge without flinching. I was also as patient with new recruits as I was with Chirayu, who was still unfortunately my line manager, even when they sent me endorsement requests on Linkedin.

But lately they had started taking me for granted. Four months without a project and the senior management had already started talking about me as though I were the Higgs-Boson particle. At one of their meetings, in fact, I had the privilege of being an X-axis item on a presentation titled 'Revenue Poopers'. Sure, I was talented and every project manager wanted a piece of me. But did that mean I had to be available at their beck and call? Or to take charge of a project, the nature of which I am even ashamed to talk about? I understand such work can be doled out to overenthusiastic trainees and summer interns by telling them this project is in keeping with the company's commitment to integrated career advancement framework, type of nonsense. But this was no way to treat an Ivy-league consultant. I am too embarrassed to give out details of this new project they were trying to thrust up my face, but suffice it to say it was like offering Shahid Kapoor's *Mausam* to Tom Hanks.

Project *Mausam* was the earliest trigger that made me seriously consider what the subscribers of my blog had been asking from me for long: that I must consider writing a book. Considering I had nothing to lose by obliging them, I finally gave an hour to Brian Jones for a web conference. With the kind of financial status of almost-nirvana that I had achieved,

I did not usually worry about spending a few thousand extra bucks here and there for miscellaneous purposes. But even the richest Indian does not mind saving on wi-fi costs as long as he can help it.

In that true spirit, I booked a conference room in the office itself and blew up some company wi-fi for this meeting. It felt great, I tell you. Especially when I sent out a mail to Chirayu, my line manager, and told him I was trying to clinch a deal with a prestigious client that evening and that the conference room was off limits for everyone. There was so much awe dripping in all the emails the senior management sent in response, wishing me luck and all. For a few minutes I felt guilty. Then the guilt disappeared when I remembered how much they had toyed with my peace of mind for so many years, and a little reciprocation wouldn't hurt anyone.

I logged into the conference at 6.00 p.m. sharp, revisiting some pivotal negotiation and communication skills I had picked up years ago from an issue of *Competition Success Review*: never sound desperate even if you know you have an edge; keep pushing the ball in the other person's court till he concedes that you hold the bargaining power. Excellent. That is exactly what I did when Brian logged in, exchanged basic pleasantries with me, and then started telling me how much he admired my blog posts. A key milestone achieved without having even tried, I smugly reclined in my seat and heard him out, nodding intermittently out of politeness. This was followed by the inevitable 'I really think there is a latent best-selling novelist in you, which we at Crown would like to nurture and engage with.' I could feel my pulse shoot up. But I maintained my stoic, unmoved expression and said all that was great, but what was in this entire deal for me?

'We pitch your work to publishers around the world,' he said. 'And we have a proven track record of getting plush deals for debutant authors with an average publishing contract worth $50,000...'

I quickly glanced at the glass window of the room to make sure my expressions were not giving me away. But frankly the mention of $50,000 had deposited my heart right inside my mouth. This could be the deal that could encourage me to quit the goddamn company and finally do what I was *meant* to do. This train of thought momentarily transported me back to depressing thoughts of Project *Mausam*, but I checked myself in time and returned to the conversation.

'So, what do you think?' he asked, struggling to catch some breath after an extensive pitch.

Now, *Competition Success Review* strongly recommends you step back a little from a conversation when you are approaching a point of agreement, because that is likely to up the stakes in your favour. While $50,000 sounded reasonable to me, I did not mind a slightly higher quote. So I simply shrugged in response and told Brian that while it was very nice of him to have spoken to me, I was but a deep, philosophical writer whose words were only meant to help him connect better with his own soul and that I had no intention of getting my work published. He made a sad face and said he respected my decision, thanked me and was about to log off when I stopped him. What sort of businessman was this fellow? No skills of persuasion only. I made a note to lend him *Clinching A Deal the Bytesphere Way* some day. An awfully long handbook, but I reckoned he could make good use of it.

'Wait,' I stopped him. 'I appreciate your faith in me. I will keep your request in mind and will let you know soon.'

I consulted Mehek on this development over dinner.

'No harm exploring Crown,' she said with a tone of warning. 'But make sure you hedge your risks.'

I told her I really appreciated she was now a Goldman Sachs employee, but I would very much like her to continue speaking to me in English.

'I mean, you had better think through this flicker of an idea you have got about quitting your job,' she said.

That made sense. Why would I want to quit a job anyway when I had been conveniently housing the aggressive consultant and the compassionate blogger inside me, with both living in perfect communion? A few Bytesphere lakhs by the side of $50,000 of a publishing contract did not sound objectionable at all. I only needed to mull over the time I would need to dedicate to an entire novel before giving Brian the nod.

3
Customer Delight

PROJECT *MAUSAM*. SIGH. Bytesphere had lost its mind totally. Well I guess I have no option but to share embarrassing details about this project. Otherwise you may not appreciate the real frustration inside me that ultimately propelled me to accept Brian's offer.

It started a couple of days before our web conference. I got a memo from the HR team that said: 'Please meet us at 2.00 p.m. in the Pink Orchid room to discuss a Level Zero Vitality Communique.'

I was as thrilled as I was confused. I was thrilled because it had been ages since the HR had massaged my ego by sending me a one-on-one invite. I was confused because I had no idea what a Level Zero Vitality Communique was supposed to mean. I replied, asking what on earth that last phrase was to be interpreted as. I received another email with nothing in it except a hyperlink called 'Organizational Glossary'. I called one of the HR associates to fetch details. She cut me off abruptly, saying she would explain everything at the meeting, as she had to rush to engage in a Stage Three Talent Preservation exercise at the moment. Someone on my floor reckoned this meant she had to sign off on an employee's resignation request, but he was not too sure either.

I reached the Pink Orchid room at the said time, sitting in that dark enclosure wondering why our meeting rooms had such exotic names when they were mostly used for presentations that worked like slow poison. 'Come to Lilydale Waterfalls at three this afternoon. Let its ergonomics enchant you. We will then tie you to a chair, turn on a projector and slowly weed your life out of you.' These names made little sense. As did the rest of that meeting. The two HR associates arrived almost twenty minutes later, carrying two giant posters of Fido Dido wearing a garish kurta and pyjamas.

'Republic Day celebrations,' one of them beamed, pointing at the poster's title. They wanted my feedback on the visual appeal and the power of the message.

'Frank feedback, please,' they said, 'we won't feel bad.'

Going by the hideous outfit they had made him wear, Fido Dido should have been the only one in the room with a right to feel bad. I gave them my frank feedback: that it was a good effort and they had their hearts in the right places and all that. But the colours were too loud, 'Republic' had been spelt 'Repubic' and Fido Dido looked more like Suppandi.

'Of course, of course,' they laughed as though that was exactly the intent behind that elaborate effort.

'Look, the colours are in keeping with the vibrancy in

the company,' they explained, to which I argued that some employees may not see the correlation especially given that the variable payouts for the year had been curtailed.

They ignored me and went on. 'Republic is obviously spelt wrong, but in this loud, engaging poster the error is not evident to the naked eye—except when we talk of a software company that has debugging ingrained in its genes.' This one hit me like a tornado. I started to say something, then realized the Pink Orchid would wilt before I left this room if I allowed the conversation to go on. And they still had a third point to make.

'Which is,' they continued, 'that every employee regardless of caste, creed, or appraisal rating, whether the cool Fido Dido or dunderhead Suppandi, would unite in celebrating this festival.'

I conceded defeat, apologized for giving my opinion, and asked them to come to the agenda of the meeting. They looked blankly at each other for a moment, and then remembered. The meeting started on a safe note. They asked me how my career graph was progressing and if I had any expectations from the company. I said that now they had reminded me, I had asked them to speak to HR at the company's London office for a potential transfer, about six months ago. And I had not heard back from them.

They spoke something very fast in response that went something like, 'As you know, we always consider an employee's career aspirations as long as they map optimally to the company's annual goals and easy come easy go I'd catch a grenade for you and blow it up your…'

Before I could reproduce their words and translate them

in my head, they had promptly jumped to the main agenda of the discussion.

Project *Mausam*. Even they could not conceal their awkwardness while giving out details, I swear. Dayanand Lalwani, the founder of Bytesphere, had decided to get his granddaughter married, much against her wishes. That was not too hard to imagine, because the groom was Haresh Patel, scion of Surat-based business tycoon Naresh Patel who sold some weird smelling hair oil, as I would learn in due course of time. Stock that remained unsold at the end of the day would remain on the groom's hair all year long. But Grandpa was adamant, and so Baby Lalwani struck a two-pronged deal: one, her wedding would be the grandest affair the country would ever witness; two, her groom needed better grooming. Dayanand agreed to the first point instantly and asked her to leave everything to him. Regarding the second point, he reportedly said that he was comfortable in principle with the thought, as long as Hair Oil did not object to such micro-management.

The next morning when he summoned the Bytesphere management to inform them of the wedding, everyone was very excited, because for some strange reason they all thought he was going to declare a few days off in celebration. Sensing the room's collective pulse, Lalwani took off his blazer, loosened his tie and started showering every hapless soul in the room with his personally anointed Hindi abuses. He scoffed at them for being cheap enough to imagine that he would grant them a holiday after they had displayed such shameful levels of resource under-utilization that year. Some more abuses followed, after which he declared that in order to ensure a grand ceremony for his daughter and to teach the worthless management a lesson in general, the company would appoint a team of un-utilized employees to help organize the wedding for him.

I stared at the associates, hoping they would break into giggles again and ask me to calm down because this company was not all that full of shit. They said nothing except, 'You are one of the chosen.' Noting that I had not reacted so far, they also slyly slipped in that the wedding was to be in Pune and that I would have to go to Pune for three months. Know that familiar feeling of the world around you crumbling to pieces? Or a fictitious worm wriggling its way up your legs right into your gut? That rare moment when your entire life flashes before your eyes? The first thing I remembered was the anthem of my MBA college. I had emotionally connected with it despite its tacky tune. It had taught me how to dream—often to only dream, but nonetheless a nice dream is what I had. And it did not include turning wedding organizer for the owner's granddaughter. Now I understand I may not have been an IIM-type MBA, but I still prided myself in the values my institute had imparted to me—glibness and excessive networking, even at the cost of substance and merit.

So I told them I wouldn't accept this assignment in a thousand lives, just because I had not been placed on a project for four months now. Wasn't it Chirayu's job to put me on an assignment? If he had failed to do so, why didn't they ask *him* to organize the wedding?

'He will be overseeing its execution,' they said.

'Yeah, right.'

Utter nonsense, seriously. I then told them I certainly

wouldn't go to Pune unless I got per diem reimbursements, which I was sure I would not get, because we often were not reimbursed even for legitimate projects.

The associates doused me with liberal showers of diplomacy in return, saying they completely respected my decision but were confident all the same that I would end up taking up the assignment. I looked at them, confused, and asked them how they were so sure. They giggled weirdly. I smelt a rat. So I reiterated my stand against the offer. They giggled again, got up and thanked me for my time, saying all further communication could happen later because they had to rush to a meeting with the board of directors to lock down on a name for this high priority project and to finalize modalities of daily communication on preparation and progress.

I stayed restless that entire afternoon, fidgeting uncomfortably in my seat. My mother learnt of the project and started crying. 'Everyone is getting married. You are turning thirty, and here you are, organizing weddings for other girls instead of marrying one yourself.'

I can't explain how frustrated I felt. I'd had enough, and asked Brian to join me once again on a web conference. He instantly agreed. Good, the desperation was still there. 'Please give me the details,' I said.

'We put your story out to the market,' he repeated. 'We offer a 100 per cent guarantee of your work getting published in this mad rush of new writers.'

'That is great, but how do you do that?' I asked again.

'We offer a sequential, phased out integrated framework of product-building because that is the only sustainable business model in the global literary market...'

I had to interrupt him and to tell him that while I understood he was conscious that he was conversing with a strategy consultant, it was perfectly alright for him to use simpler words because I understood them equally well.

'We offer you three grades of services,' he broke his pitch down, much to my relief. 'The elementary package, the augmented package, and the customer delight package.'

I leaned forward to listen more intently. We were finally getting somewhere.

'The Elementary Package will cost you $1200,' he continued. 'We will pick up your completed manuscript and pitch it to our network of trusted publishers around the globe. We guarantee a positive turnaround in under twelve months.'

'I agree,' I said, unable to contain my excitement any more. Project *Mausam* had upset the wiring in my brain.

'There is more,' he said, raising his hand with a smile. 'Sign up with us for the Augmented Package for $2000, and we will also edit and refine your manuscript and furnish a delectable, marketable product to publishers.'

My pulse shot up a little more. 'And the Customer Delight Package?'

'We help you choose everything—a commercially viable storyline, we help you with your character graphs and motives, conflict and resolution, and THEN we pitch your work to the publishers,' he spoke in a single breath, then reached for a glass of water lying near him, and then added: 'This Customer Delight Package can be offered at a discounted rate of $3000.'

I did a quick math and then reached for a glass of water

myself. He called this kind of price *customer delight*? I expressed my reservations about the cost, to which he explained that the fear of extravagance should not come in the way of furnishing one's debut product. Just so that he would not form a poor impression about me, I casually let him know that I was actually a platinum holder of three Mastercard credit cards and that I probably paid more taxes annually than what his Customer Delight Package would cost me. But at the same time, I was prudent about my choices and confident about my writing skills (as my blog subscribers would testify). And so it was decided: I would work on my manuscript independently, and then let them have a go at pitching it to the right publisher.

'I look forward to seeing you at the symposium in March,' he said.

'I have not made up my mind about attending it yet,' I said.

'You don't want to miss it,' he warned. 'You'll meet some interesting writers there.'

'Will I?' I had never heard of these symposiums before.

'Of course,' he laughed just before signing off. 'That symposium only selects the very best!'

I maintained a calm smile until I was signed out of the web conference. Then I sprang out of my seat, stepped on to the table, took off my shirt and waved it in the air, and then put it on back when I saw Chirayu walk towards the conference room.

'I am running late. I have to wrap up work and then pick up my daughter from the mall,' he spoke like the wind. 'I have fired some prints of a voucher for her free violin lessons. Please get them to my desk.'

I still find it hard to believe this happened, but I stood my ground in response and shook my head.

'Get the prints!' he ordered.

'They are your daughter's violin lessons,' I shrugged. 'Why don't you go get them yourself?'

I wish I could have photographed the dog's face. A cocktail of shock, awe and shame flushed across his fat cheeks as I settled in a chair and whistled softly. This company was not going to take me for granted any more. I would be calling the shots now. If they didn't like what they got, I always had a novel to write instead.

4

We Are the Frooti Boys

THE NEXT MORNING I went to Chirayu's cabin, apologized for my misbehaviour the previous evening and asked him if he would like me to pick his daughter up after her violin classes and drop her home if he was keeping supremely busy. The bastard agreed.

Look, I am not the kind of person who forms a vision and then steps off a predetermined path. I was entirely sure until the previous night that it would not suffice for me to just decline Project *Mausam*. I needed to teach this organization a lesson it would never forget—in the form of my resignation. But when I'd gone to Mehek's new company-sponsored sea-facing apartment the previous night (I wanted to jump into that tempting jacuzzi in her building, but I told her I wanted to help her move her luggage etcetera), she did not sound too happy about my intention to quit. Why not, I asked her; was my love not enough for her, and so on? So that she could rub it in a good bit, she said she didn't care about my finances because she was 'reasonably self-sufficient thanks to Goldman Sachs', which was a polite way of telling me that my monthly salary was probably what she was in a position to actually spend every month, 'but my concern is that it might be too early, don't you think?' she asked.

I explained that only people who were afraid of swimming tested the water first; I was a free-spirited dolphin that just wanted to jump in and get wet.

'I don't mind,' she finally said. 'But you know Dad, don't you?'

Yes, I knew her Dad. Supercop Gupta. The great robber of my peace of mind in a policeman's clothes. We had not got off to a perfect start, him and I, for various reasons such as my upset stomach the first time he met me, his cheap and tasteless jokes targeted at me, and his general rubbishing of anything that I said. But over time, as Mehek told me, he had conceded that Mehek was madly in love with me and that he or her mother could do very little to convince her otherwise. So they were slowly trying to accept me, no, actually they were slowly trying to stop humiliating me on schedule. And Mehek feared that any new surprises such as a career renunciation would promptly upset the apple cart. I sighed over the kind of things I had to do as a part of my social obligations for love. More importantly, this conversation later influenced me to mend my fences with Chirayu and periodically (nearly every day) pick up his daughter after her violin classes.

'That is not all,' she told me.

So basically, her first cousin was expecting her first baby in Mysore, and she had been invited to the ceremony but with strict instructions that she should bring me along. Having, with great difficulty, somewhat swallowed the fact that I was their only likely candidate for a son-in-law, her parents had projected me before all their relatives as a superhero in the geekdom of Bytesphere, with the magic ability to shoot dollar bills off his wrists. In the true spirit of Indian relatives who got turned on by the wealth quotient of someone they had never seen before, the clan had now made it mandatory for me to attend this baby shower.

'Why don't we drive down?' she suggested excitedly. 'Maybe take a nice detour in Goa for a couple of days, and then further on to Mysore?'

I reckoned that would be a good idea. For one, we could take my flashy new Hyundai Sonata out for a nice road trip and drive Mehek's family crazy on seeing my car. Two, our sex life had gotten very gloomy ever since Mehek had joined Goldman Sachs, because for some strange reason the company had mandated all employees to attend an in-house yoga class every morning at six, which meant all our collective sexual energy could be thrown out of her French window.

And so it was decided. I would do this one hell of a road trip. And I would keep my job, despite seeing the pointlessness of it all. But that would still not stop me from disallowing those HR associates to put me on to that role of planning a goddamn wedding. I would politely, firmly and very lucidly write them an email the next morning, stating valid, solid reasons for declining the project. The next morning I reached work early and saw this piece of crap in my inbox:

From: Pallavi Das (HRD)
To: Nakul Kapoor
Cc: Anita Kumar (HRD); Chirayu Chaudhary; Anand Rai; Board_of_Directors; Team_Wedding Project

Subject: The Wedding Project –Induction

Dear Nakul,

As discussed at length yesterday, we are pleased to induct you to The Wedding Project with effect from today. You will be working in the core team focused towards a seamless conduction of all planned ceremonies as part of Aditi Lalwani's wedding with Haresh Patel. Please make it convenient to attend a briefing session and formal kick-off (tea and biscuits will be served) with the board of directors today at 3.00 p.m. All communication regarding your reporting project manager and the division of responsibilities will be relayed in this meeting. Thank you for accepting this challenging project. We are confident your proven consulting and interfacing skills will be leveraged to show yet another project the gateway to success.

In case you have any doubts around the project, please call the HR helpline between 2.00–2.20 p.m. on Tuesdays and Thursdays.

Pallavi
HR Associate,
Bytesphere Inc.

Ok, so this was a little upsetting. Clearly there had been some confusion. My state of mind was very volatile, but I was pretty sure I had not given my nod to participate in this project much as I tried to remember. Luckily, I had recently turned patron to Sri Sri Ravishankar's terrific sermons on The Art of Living, which told me that the human mind was susceptible to ghastly errors when pissed off. Give people the benefit of doubt and sort out misunderstandings by way of amicable communication. I gave it some time. Went over to get a cup of coffee. Then I typed out a very contained response.

> From: Nakul Kapoor
> To: Pallavi Das (HRD)
> Cc: Anita Kumar (HRD)
>
> Subject: Re: The Wedding Project–Induction
>
> *Hi Pallavi, this email is a little disconcerting. Can you please advise on what basis you deemed my response to yesterday's discussion as that of 'acceptance'? I am not willing to join this project at any cost. Please suggest a suitable time we can meet today to clear any confusion and take appropriate corrective measures. Thanks.*
>
> *Nakul Kapoor*

~

From: Pallavi Das (HRD)
To: Nakul Kapoor; Anita Kumar (HRD)

Subject: Out of Office Re: The Wedding Project–Induction

Hi,

We are currently out of office in connection with preparations for the flag hoisting ceremony as part of the Republic Day celebrations. If your mail is to volunteer for the event, please leave your number and we will get back to you. For all other HR related queries, please contact our HR helpdesk between 2.00–2.20 p.m. on Tuesdays and Thursdays. Or you could direct any urgent matters to Meenakshi Reddy, head of HR operations. Thanks!

~

Sri Sri Ravishankar's tips were losing their potency. I don't think they accounted for situations when the adversary was hell bent on bringing out the devil inside you. Well, one final chance maybe.

From: Nakul Kapoor
To: Meenakshi Reddy (HRD)

Subject: Fwd: Out of Office Re: The Wedding Project–Induction

Hi Meenakshi,

Please see email below. As much as you can imagine my situation, I must emphasize I am being forced into this project against my will, which is in violation with our 'Sanctity of Employee Preferences' clause. Request your kind intervention at the earliest. Thanks.

Nakul Kapoor

~

From: Meenakshi Reddy (HRD)

To: Nakul Kapoor

Subject: Out of Office Re: Fwd: Out of Office Re: The Wedding Project – Induction

Hi, I can't attend to your emails right now as I am in Belgium attending a conference on 'Enhancement of Employee Relations: The Value of Open Communication'. Please direct all HR queries to either Pallavi Das or Anita Kumar. Also please consider this email a reminder to fill out your self-appraisal before the 20th of January, failing which you will not be eligible for your variable payouts this quarter. Thanks.

Meenakshi

~

I felt fire in my eyes. An overpowering itch all over. The hackles on my forearms rose and swayed wildly like paddy fields. My skin was turning crimson by the second. Rage was taking control of me. I rushed to the bathroom and splashed some cold water on my face even as I watched my canine teeth turn into sharp blades.

Chirayu entered the bathroom to take a leak, and shrieked like a little child on watching me metamorphose. 'You all will pay!' my bloodied eyes said to him.

'All it takes is a quick chat,' he convinced me to follow him to his cabin.

Coffee and cookies were called for. Starbucks! Not bad. At least he knew how to raise his standards under pressure. I was made to eat, after which I calmed down a little. Chirayu explained this was a very prestigious assignment because it challenged me to expand my horizons. Luckily for him, this was spoken while a delicious Oreo cookie was still dissolving in my mouth. He conjured some more tricks to convince me: accommodation at the best hotel in Pune, a chauffer-driven car, reasonable work hours. The desperation was palpable. I began to lean in, only to see how far they were willing to bend. Just when I thought he had finally learnt how to make a good pitch, he picked up a marker and proceeded to his whiteboard. He drew four stick diagrams of a man who looked more like an ape man, which was fine assuming he pictured himself as he drew. The four monkey-men were arranged concentrically and scores of little arrows jutted out in all directions around them, like Alfred Hitchcock's *Birds*. Then he said I must not pay heed to the HR's nonsensical, verbose sermons and must just align my decisions based on this theory he was trying to explain to me. He wrote the title on the board: *The Apocalyptical Circle of Flawed Strategy*. Propounded by a Mongolian strategist Jung Boo, it seemed. And then, as he continued writing some nonsense about the theory, his marker ran out of ink. He asked me to go fetch a marker from one of the adjacent conference rooms on the floor. I went to each of the conference rooms, picked up their markers, threw them in the trash chute, and came back and told him there was no marker. He appeared crestfallen. I tried appearing likewise and insisted he summarize it for me in one sentence.

'You have no choice but to go to Pune,' he said, and then added he had already emailed me a list of documents that I could read to get familiar with what was going to be expected of me.

I played my last card. 'Alright, but I want per diem reimbursements while in Pune.'

'Speak to Meenakshi,' he shrugged, and thus the discussion ended.

At that point, I had little energy to get into an argument. I returned to my desk instead, set my internal messenger status to 'Do not disturb', and then started writing my story.

I had read up a lot of online articles about writing a debut novel and the roadblocks one was likely to encounter en route. Frankly I thought the entire tone of struggle about writing a story was grossly exaggerated. And writer's block? Please. That was a lame excuse for plain laziness. A clear idea was all it took to get started. It would be a simple story of a diligent, genius consultant stuck in a company filled with idiots. I had examples all around me. I wrote with rage and passion. The prose and paragraphs flowed seamlessly. It was like I had cut my heart open and was bleeding into those words. This magic lasted for only twenty minutes, after which I found myself staring at a blank page and at my watch. Forty minutes before that dreadful brief about 'The Wedding Project'. No wonder I was losing my concentration. Writing required mental bandwidth, which in my case was clogged by the thought of running around Lalwani's granddaughter to arrange for the measurements of her wedding dress. I would have to put it off until later that night.

The time left before the meeting was spent on creating my brand—as Brian had rightly advised, people must know the writer well before they know his words. Because I was not the kind of person who would go overboard trying to fish for compliments, I decided to keep it subtle with a simple Facebook update: 'Interesting times ahead. Selected for the Young Turks Literary Symposium in Zurich. Next is what?'

I got myself a cup of coffee from the pantry and returned to find forty-three likes on the status. The funny thing about friends is you tend to forget they exist until you suddenly gain acclaim at the international level and become some sort of phenomenon when they come back and say hello and all that. I didn't really mind that. Except I had three comments as well, asking for tips on writing. This is what I really disliked. When would people realize that art is not something one can master by seeking tips? What nonsense. Writers are born, not created. The biggest tip ever on writing is that you sit down and write. Everyone starts asking for tips without showing intent. I did not want to be impolite. So I just pretended I had not read those questions and went off to attend the meeting.

Inside that depressing meeting room, my ambitions had started dying a slow death at the hands of Chirayu and two others like him from the senior management. Four chairs were placed on one side of the table, I sat in one slouched, indifferent. One seat lay unoccupied. The two chairs on either side of me were taken by employees named, believe it or not, Karan and Arjun. I never figured which one was which, but it was not important. Our wavelengths did not match. They were roughly my age but clearly half my experience and maturity. I could tell from the way they were eyeing the tetrapacks of Frooti lying on their tables. To balance out this gross misbehaviour, they had also opened the free stationery packs handed to them and were pretending they could not wait to start taking notes the moment someone would start speaking.

'What do you think constitutes a great marriage?' Bala, one of the two other managers, asked. Karan instantly wrote 'Key Elements of A Good Marriage' on his notepad and underlined it twice before taking a large slurp of his Frooti. The sound of saliva mixing with mango juice reverberated through the room. By now of course, I was fully awake and completely unwilling to answer this ridiculous question. But the voice grew stronger and more streamlined in my direction. The face got clearer too, as it approached me. Bala, the company's finance head, rarely gave an audience, except for very critical meetings. Such as this one.

He repeated his question. 'What do you think constitutes a good marriage?'

I was tempted to answer 'Sexual chemistry' so I could be thrown out of this bullshit for my profanity and in the process be spared the horror of humiliating my career with this blip on the screen. But a tiny voice in my head reminded me of a bonus due in less than four months, which was an amount worth respecting and keeping shut for.

So I silently muttered, 'Faith', not because it made sense but because it was the first safe word that occurred to me.

Bala looked victorious. 'Very good! Wow! Faith!' The remaining people in the room nodded vigorously as Bala ran to the whiteboard and wrote the F-word. After which he turned to me again, as though the other two fellows did not even exist, asking, 'What else?'

How do I know what else, saala? I was thirty, I was not married, and given my recent circumstances I was not likely to learn much about marriage in the near future. Karan, who had been taking notes so as to avoid eye contact with his quizmaster, had finally finished his Frooti and had nowhere else to look but right into Bala's eyes.

'Good understanding,' he mumbled. Bala reluctantly replicated this generic answer on the whiteboard, and still demanded, 'What else?'

Karan added 'Compatibility' and 'Social Equanimity', which elicited some acknowledgement from the board. So he got hyper and also added 'Spiritual Connect' which almost sent everyone into peals of laughter. Bala looked very unhappy because he was looking for a 'very specific answer which you guys haven't thought of yet.'

Arjun hadn't spoken yet, but when Bala gave up on us and finally scribbled something on the board that made me lose faith in the importance of coherent communication, Arjun almost jumped out of his seat and sighed, 'Actually, I was just about to say that.'

What was Bala's question? 'What constitutes a good marriage?'

What was Bala's answer?

This.

'HOLISTIC FLAVOUR OF COMMUNION.' (And Arjun was just about to say that. Minus marks to him already).

'Because,' as was explained to us over a thousand laborious presentations, 'an Indian marriage is not between two people, but between two families, and every element of a wedding plan makes it count.'

A slew of lectures followed by Bala and the other manager, even as Chirayu impatiently fidgeted in his seat, itching to speak. The presentations began with something that was titled 'What is holistic communion and what role do we play?' The assault on our senses reached a crescendo when Chirayu came to the dais to start speaking on 'The Wedding Project—Key Result Areas'. Just then, Raghav Krishnan walked in and occupied that fourth chair next to us that had stayed vacant for most part of the session.

Raghav was introduced as our project manager for this prestigious assignment, a whiz in corporate strategy, a sucker for statistical and quantitative analysis, and a hater of powerpoint presentations. For the first time in all these years, someone in the company had had the gall to ask a presenter to stop speaking and to switch off the projector lights. Chirayu looked like his lungs had been forked out. Raghav had won my faith already. He declared he had only ten spare minutes and would like to be briefed in that time about project details, his role and the expectations from his team. He also laid out rules: all communication to his core team, which was the three of us, would be routed only through him, because, 'I know how to weed out unnecessary details.'

The meeting ended prematurely. I clearly saw Chirayu's eyes filled with giant tears as we left the room. That made me very happy. Raghav, meanwhile, reconvened with Karan, Arjun and me outside the room and implored us to unlearn all the hogwash that had been doled out to us on the projector. He likened presentations to carbohydrates, which he thought were the most unnecessary element on everyone's dietary chart and added no nutritional value.

I observed him carefully for the first time, this man had abs, clearly. I could see the ripped torso through the pinstriped shirt. And his taut jawline was enhanced by just the right amount of grey forming on his sideburns. Full George Clooney kind of stuff. Finally, a role model one could look up to. I needed to spend more time with Raghav. I wanted to be like Raghav. I was just about to engage him in some meaningful conversation about the draft roadmap of 'The Wedding Project' when Arjun ruined the ambience by asking aloud how best he could summarize his role in this assignment if he were to put it on his CV for another job. And then quickly added 'Hypothetically speaking.'

This pissed off Raghav no end. He snipped the conversation short, told us to distribute the responsibilities of catering, guest lodging and amusement, and venue logistics between the three of us. We would send weekly progress reports to him for his review and assessment, and he would provide feedback on how quality could be bettered by containing costs. I promptly called the dibs on catering, because I had a long standing experience on telling exquisite cuisine from mediocre nonsense. Poor Arjun was not given a choice; Raghav imposed guest lodging and amusement on him and suggested he could title his CV's bullet point 'Social engagement for a client using unique human capital tools'. Strangely, Karan jotted this on his notepad too, right below 'Venue logistics—the Bytesphere way'.

Later that evening, I found Raghav's cabin and pretended to take some prints right outside his working bay. Then I bumped into him and said it would be very exciting to spend more time with him because we shared a penchant for hunting meaning and purpose through statistics in business decisions, unlike most others around us. It was only five, but he had packed up for the day already (I wondered for a minute if he was on a half-day). He offered to catch up for dinner over one weekend, maybe at the Hyatt (what the fuck) because he stayed only a stone's throw away and was a privileged guest there (WHAT THE FUCK). I agreed, saying although I personally preferred the sushi bar at the Taj, the Hyatt wouldn't hurt for a change.

I returned home that night and wrote some more, amidst intermittent breaks during which I watched multiple episodes of *How I Met Your Mother*. I was amazed it had taken me five seasons to note how hot Robin Scherbatsky was. Three episodes later, I realized I had written enough for the day and it would be wise to take it slow and easy, so I could savour this writing process rather than labour over it. I stayed awake that entire night and finished watching all the remaining seasons. Robin Scherbatsky looked better with every episode. What an amazing night. Refreshing and invigorating. I was ready to take on the challenges that lay ahead.

5

A Favour for A Eurail Pass

I COULD NOT find a polite way of telling Brian that I was fed up of attending these web conferences with him. And that he should quit strangulating my creativity by following up with me on the status of my work every forty-eight hours. So I simply called him one day and told him I was to go off to Pune the next morning on a critical official mission and that I would be unreachable for the next month or two, and that we would directly have our next conversation three months later with my completed manuscript on his desktop. He sounded satisfied and left me alone for the next month.

I fixed up that Hyatt dinner with Raghav one night before going off on holiday.

'My only condition is I will foot the bill,' I insisted.

We then got into that customary argument over the bill, and he said he was obliged to pay because he was senior to me (maybe a subtle allusion to the salary gradient). Jumping to my own defence, I clarified I kept dining at these buffets every now and then and it was not a big deal for me at all. He finally agreed.

It was not in my nature to socialize with colleagues from work. But Raghav was different. He was very supportive when I told him I would be on leave for a week starting the next day.

'As long as you get the job done, I don't care,' he said.

He was also very supportive when I told him I would be off to Zurich for a week, just ten days ahead of the big wedding. There was an entire team to cover up for me, he assured me. What a wonderful manager. Why could he not be my line manager instead of Chirayu? At dinner, we forgot all about work and got chatting about common interests. Impressed by my selection at the symposium and the forthcoming contract for a novel (with a leading publisher whose name I cannot disclose, I added), he told me he was fascinated by literature and by people with creative pursuits. Because no one at Bytesphere usually said such kind things about fellow employees, it took me some time to absorb the fact that he meant this seriously. He told me he was an avid reader himself and had often contemplated writing.

'But it is nice to meet someone who actually had the guts,' he said.

I went into a tizzy with that compliment but given my humility that has always helped me stay grounded and focused, I simply nodded and smiled. He suggested we order some sushi before digging into the buffet, because it was to die for. I nodded vehemently and then quickly glanced at the menu.

Four fucking thousand rupees for a bowl of sushi. I did not have a problem paying for it; I simply cringed at the thought that I must have been the first North Indian who would spend

Rs 4000 on a food product the size of a one rupee coin. Well, at least it tasted nice. We ordered some more, and then some more, as we got talking about books and authors. Raghav told me he thought I had the potential to make a great story-teller (I don't know why), but he added, 'I especially noted this when you were talking to me about your theories on human resource retention at work yesterday.' He said he was keen to wait and watch if I crossed that fine line between writing and expressing, and that would be the single biggest achievement he would be looking to see in my book.

Everything was going great so far. His sentences were sometimes too deep and intense for me to absorb, but I was able to resonate with him to a reasonable extent. But then once we got our food from the buffet, the kind of things he started asking me completely baffled me. There was nothing wrong with his questions. They were probably profound and intellectual on various levels. But the truth was that I was not much of a reader. I had simply come to be this immensely loved, popular blogger for the sheer simplicity and honesty with which I shared my expressions. My impending surge to literary stardom was purely incidental. But I did not want to come across as callous before him, so I tried responding with answers as accurate and sensible as possible.

For example, he asked, 'Do you think the writings of the Renaissance period still make a ripple effect felt on modern literature?'

I obviously had no idea what ripples were created by literature during Renaissance, if any. I was just about to tell him I avoided reading because I feared as a writer I would be influenced by others' writing styles.

But just then he added, 'Quoting the very remarkable Twain "the man who does not read has no significant advantage over the man who cannot read".'

So I simply stated that while the Renaissance had a deep impact on people's credos and popular culture, literature was tangential to the time constant and evolved at its own pace and every era of art carried with it an independent perspective of the world.

He looked a little unsettled by my answer. 'I did not get you. Please explain?'

I argued this logic could not be articulated, it could only be felt. An awkward silence followed. We got dessert and worked on it rather quietly. Then he asked me who my favourite writers from the Renaissance period were, just to be sure he was talking to the right guy. I signalled to the steward for the bill, and then said it was not appropriate of me to label authors as favourites or second-fiddle because that would be belittling the causes for which they wrote and anyway prose was too qualitative and opulent to be rated and maybe we should leave now that the bill had been paid and it was getting really late.

As we prepared to part ways, Raghav received a call that lasted about three minutes. But it had clearly lasted long enough to have taken the wind out of him. I asked him if something was wrong. He declined to comment, saying it was something personal and he would not want to bother me with. I offered to at least walk him home. Poor Raghav, under that veneer of that smooth operator, he couldn't conceal his vulnerability. He promptly changed the subject, wished me luck for my assignment in Pune, and assured me that as long as I worked smart and kept him in the loop on all updates, I would have nothing to worry about as far as the project was concerned. I wished I could reciprocate such assurance, if only he spoke up about what was it that had bothered him.

'Maybe I can be of some help?' I asked again.

He opened up to me gradually. His cousin had duped him of his rightful share of some old ancestral land. He was now not only stripped of a good chunk of his familial wealth but also needed additional investments to engage a good lawyer who could bail him out of his trouble. I asked him if I could lend him some money. He hesitated, but I insisted.

'Only for the interim,' I assured him, asking how much he'd like.

After a lot of formality, he said he would accept one lakh from me, but would repay me the day this case saw the end of the day. I said he could take his time; one lakh was a very small amount for the position I was at and I wouldn't even realize it was missing.

We shook hands and parted for the day. I had never thought I would say this about someone bred in the Bytesphere management, but it was the beginning of a very solid friendship.

I returned home and was struck by an epiphany. It was futile to try writing at home. There were just too many distractions—Robin Scherbatsky, the television remote lying right next to me, random Youtube videos. I was more of the outdoors-inspired artist who sourced inspiration from people around him, by observing them. It would have to be a café hereon; a nice cup of coffee and a comfortable ambience. Perfect. It was worth holding off on that story for another night, after all.

My Facebook update about the selection at the symposium now had a hundred and sixty-nine likes! Brian was right. There was value in creating a brand ahead of creating the product. I went through all the comments: flattering and inspiring all at once. I thanked each one of them personally, except this one long lost classmate from undergrad days who posted this:

> Hey brother, very proud of you. Hey if you don't mind can you carry a small parcel for my cousin in Geneva? It is just two hours from Zurich. I can pay for your Eurail ticket, thanks.

I was too tired to react. I just went off to sleep. An exciting (except the part where I would meet the in-laws) road trip beckoned.

6
....
Maps Will Guide You Home

THE ROAD TRIP began very pathetically. Here I was, trying to make it all special for her by juggling between the roles of a driver and that of the in-vehicle DJ. And she picked up a fight over nothing. We must have barely hit the highway to Goa, and instead of taking in the serene beauty of the Western Ghats interspersed with uninspiring seweries, she started giving me instructions about how to behave with her relatives.

'Please do not say anything embarrassing there,' was one of her instructions, I present as a sample for you. What insane paranoia was this, I asked her. Was I a child? If anything, she needed to be assured by the fact that I struck up easy and lucid communication with people of all demographics, as she would have amply seen while working under me at Bytesphere. But she claimed her relatives were cut from a different cloth and were not easy to impress.

'So what do you need from me exactly?' I asked her.

She said she just wanted to lay out a context before me of what her relatives were like and what kind of discussions and probing I would need to gear myself up for before meeting them. I asked her if she would like me to download Microsoft Visio so that she could draw me a flow diagram that lucidly described the interpersonal dynamics between all her relatives.

'You don't need to get nasty,' she snapped.

A good part of the remaining drive was fairly turbulent. Only the sound of chips being munched on, and the aggressive switching of songs on the player. Finally at a pit stop I apologized and told her how much I was looking forward to meeting her relatives, especially her father, and then she eased up for the next twenty-four hours. We reached Goa and booked a nice, romantic cottage by Calangute beach. I personally would have preferred booking us a suite at Cidade de Goa, but she was sometimes extraordinarily prudent about expenses. The cottage wasn't bad either. We lit candles, scented the room with Ayurvedic perfumes, and made love. It was fabulous, not so much for the ambience as for the fact that for a change she did not get a phone call from Aniket while we were having sex. (I had never met this colleague of hers, but I pre-emptively felt very sorry for him because she had told me he had a mild crush on her. When he realized he didn't stand a chance otherwise, he had now started messaging her almost daily seeking mentorship and what not). Once she was asleep, I took my laptop to the nearest shack, ordered coffees on schedule, and wrote through the night.

Two mornings later, we were on the road to Mysore, when we got into a bigger fight. While setting out from Mumbai, she had vetoed my suggestion of using a GPS to drive down and had insisted we use a map instead like proper backpacking tourists, 'because maps are romantic yaar.' I had told her I would find it a little difficult to drive while referring to the map alongside. She had assured me she would guide me along the way and that I should 'just enjoy the drive yaar.' Which I did all the way till Goa, and also for the first nineteen hours of our drive towards Mysore, until around 1.00 a.m. in the morning when we entered a village where everyone seemed to be speaking a language that sounded like Tulu.

I calmly asked her to check the map once again, because I humbly thought we had gone wrong somewhere. At this point she started crying loudly, saying we were in a village some eight kilometres away from Mangalore. There wasn't a doubt in my mind at this stage that the blame would somehow shift on me. So I played it very safe by patting her comfortingly as I drove her down to a *dhaba* and poured some cold lassi down her throat. Exactly with the same calmness as I always handled my university results, I then gently told her this was exactly why I preferred the GPS over the map. THAT WAS ALL. Nothing more. In a most bizarre move, she stood up and left in a huff, and began walking down the highway saying she was going home and it was her fault she chose an exotic holiday for us.

So then I began following her in my car like a total idiot, trying to convince her to stop the drama and come finish her lassi (because that luscious looking Tandoori Chicken we had left at the dhaba was going to be the only memorable part of the trip). Some onlookers, of whom it is typical never to mind their own business, somehow thought I was trying to stalk her, following her like that slowly in my car. So they rained down on me and were almost about to kill me, when thankfully good sense prevailed and she came to my rescue. Then she silently walked back towards the dhaba, I silently took a U-turn and followed her back to the dhaba as those onlookers had a good laugh at these shameful proceedings. After having devoured the only remaining gulab jamun in that dhaba that I had initially laid my eyes on, she told me she was extremely upset to discover that I was a self-centred man who never bothered about her needs. I stared at her, dumbfounded, and so she angrily explained she had clearly specified she wanted a National Geographic map for the trip and I still went and got her a cheaper unbranded map from some stationery store. At first, I laughed uproariously in response, assuming this was a joke meant to try and diffuse the tension of the moment. But she hadn't smiled. So I asked her to stop being so absurd, because a map of any other brand would read just the same and this could not possibly have been responsible for her guiding us to this strange village in the middle of the night. She snubbed me for trying to change the topic and declared that the key takeaway from the entire trip was that I was a selfish, irresponsible man who never really tried to understand her mind and that if I was like this already how could she expect me to suddenly mature into a Mohnish Bahl of *Hum Saath Saath Hain* after marriage? Another 19 hours and 250 litres of petrol later, not only had I apologized to her profusely, I had also made note never to use logic in any argument with her again.

By the time we reached Mysore I had lost a lot of energy trying to calm her down. So I did not have much resolve left to try and be socially presentable and friendly with everyone. But when my Sonata pulled into the porch of her uncle's house, approximately eighty relatives streamed out of the main door to greet us and I was left with little choice but to smile sweetly and allow all the cousins to take pictures with me and my car. It took me fifteen minutes to be able to make it to the front door, where Mehek's parents stood waiting for us. Mummy Gupta was cordial in her greetings. She smiled, said some nice things about how much she had been looking forward to seeing me. But Daddy Gupta just stood examining me as though I were a convict. He saw the bouquet in my hand which, by the way, was obviously for the to-be mother in the house. But he snatched it, muttering 'I don't like formalities' before tossing it on the shoe rack lying in the foyer. Bloody nonsense, I don't like you! He had to be pretty darn pompous to imagine I'd buy him, of all people, ANYTHING at all. As it is, he didn't have a particularly beautiful face. Top it with the arrogance, I noticed he was wearing cufflinks that had 'IPS' carved on them just in case, I doubt he would ever get a bouquet even if he walked into a flower boutique and paid for one.

In the thirty seconds that we were alone in the foyer, he undressed me with his eyes shamelessly, grimacing as he examined the bulges near my waist. Thankfully one of the cousins came right then and dragged Mehek and me towards the dining table which had been thronged by the rest of the clan.

'Here they are, here they are,' everyone started chanting as they came forward to hug Mehek and to, for some reason, touch me like I was a roast turkey whose tenderness needed to be checked. Random whispers such as 'Why is his nose crooked?' and 'He must be at least 85 kilos, no?' reached my ears to temporarily unsettle me. But I quickly regained my sense of composure by recalibrating the method with which I would need to blend into this new group and break ice with them. The answer was obvious: I would rely on my trusted fallback mechanism of deploying my sense of humour. Once the opportunity presented itself, of course. Until then I followed Mehek's cue, arched my back and swept the floor in a neat circle, accumulating the blessings of everyone whose feet my fingers ended up grazing in the process.

This ordeal ended when the elder daughter finally arrived in the room—her beautiful glow belied the inevitable extra weight she had gained. She strode towards me with a smile. I seized the opportunity, shook hands with her in congratulations and said, gesturing towards her loosely covered belly, 'You, little one, have had a gorgeous young lady wage a battle against the weighing machine. We can't wait any longer for you to pop out!'

Suddenly everyone in the room stopped talking. I looked around, confused: what part of that joke was so difficult to understand and appreciate? And why was the to-be mother… wait, why was she beginning to cry… no, wail… no, storm out of the room angrily? I looked at Mehek for a sign, but she had her face dug in her hands. One of the relatives then held me by the shoulders and beckoned me to sit, explaining that the girl I had just spoken to was the younger, unmarried daughter and that she was not pregnant by any measure and that I had touched upon a very delicate nerve by making a joke about her weight.

I looked at Mehek helplessly, trickles of sweat running down my legs fervently; it turned out the context setting had not been adequate after all. Seriously, what was Mehek thinking when she left out important details about what the younger daughter's situation was? Unnecessary cause of embarrassment, this. Seeing me stutter, the girl's father took pity on me and tried to placate me by saying it was not my fault at all; their daughter had put on some weight lately which may have caused the confusion. In fact, her mother added, they had been on the lookout for a suitable match for her but she was a little distressed by the whole 'slim and beautiful' requirement.

Seriously what was going on? What was wrong with this family? I admit I was not the right person at that point of time to question the intent of the mother's remarks, but what was the point of discussing a plump girl's weight in front of an entire gathering? We heard the daughter wailing even louder from the room inside. Because I was accustomed to dealing with tricky situations such as client escalations and dialogue deadlocks, I volunteered to go inside and make her feel better. Her father looked at me somewhat sceptically and volunteered to accompany me inside even as the others watched with bated breaths.

With the hopes of an entire family pinned on me, I gingerly stepped into her room, her father trailing me, uttering her name in soft whispers as though he were calling a goat out of hiding. We found her in a corner, clutching her sauna belt and trying hard to suppress her sobs. Her father pleaded with her not to make a scene before everyone else and that the function was due to start any minute. But she would not relent. So I went up to her and compassionately told her not to be disheartened or to think that someone's weight could be an impediment to finding one's true life partner.

'Have faith,' I patted her comfortingly. 'Trust me, I have

seen all sorts of people get married in the recent past. It's no big deal.'

She started crying again. I was exasperated. Her father dragged me out of the room and led me back to the dining area. By now, the elder daughter, who was actually pregnant, had also arrived at the gathering. But I decided to play it safe and said absolutely nothing to her. Dinner was served, after which, the hosts announced, there would be games that everyone would have to participate in. I did not want to play any games. I just wanted food, and some rest maybe, after that extremely long drive. Most of all, I just wanted this function to end so I could go deposit myself in a corner where I would not be judged for any and everything I spoke.

So after dinner, as the younger brigade played a bunch of very noisy games, the elders ushered me into a quiet room and gave me company. Now you can imagine this was even more awkward, because there were maybe twenty of us holed up in a room and the awkwardness of the episode with the younger daughter was still fresh. Daddy Gupta had finished singing praises of my career accomplishments, some of which bordered on exaggeration. There was now little left to talk about and I reckoned we would be in that room for at least another hour till those wretched games ended. Desperate to strike conversation, I chanced upon a framed photograph of a certain *LT SETHJI GUPTA* hung on the wall right behind Daddy Gupta's younger brother, the host of the evening.

I began with what was a safe assumption. 'Mehek's grandfather?'

The uncle nodded. He was about to say something when

I clucked my tongue and said, 'How I wish he were here with us today.'

Daddy Gupta sank into his chair and closed his eyes. Mummy Gupta nearly fainted.

'What do you mean?' the uncle asked. 'He *is* with us.'

'Of course, of course,' I nodded. 'Their blessings never leave us, years after…'

'He is alive!' Daddy Gupta cut me short with a little sigh.

All eyes turned to something standing behind me. I turned behind. LT SETHJI GUPTA stood over my head, in flesh and blood, defying all logic around the prefix "LT".

'Lala Tribhuvandas *Sethji* Gupta,' he sneered.

What sort of ugly ploy to embarrass me was this? I looked around the room, angry and confused. Why would someone abbreviate one's first name and insert *Sethji* just to confuse the living hell out of someone who was visiting the family for the first time?

'*Sethji* is his moniker,' someone whispered.

'Nakul, we need to leave,' Daddy Gupta hissed. 'You must be tired.'

Damn right, we needed to leave. I was tired. And I was fed up. We crashed at Daddy Gupta's official bungalow. I tried drowning out voices from the adjacent room, but 'I hope Mehek knows what she is getting into' did not escape my sharp ears. Well. All questions would be answered. I would let my book do the talking. But first, I needed to get that Wedding Project out of my way to regain my lost peace of mind.

7

Hareshji Aa Gaye, Hareshji Aa Gaye

PUNE WAS MUCH more fun than I had thought. I was put up at Paradise Resort, one of the premier luxury hotels in the city. The project was not too bad either. Yes, it was hectic, because I had but one month on hand, and practically every restaurateur was making a beeline to win the catering contract. For the first week, I had had little time to plan my meetings. I spent most of my time on the field, scheduling breakfast sampling sessions with the smaller vendors, and lunch and dinner banquets with the Goliaths of the food business. At the end of the second week, I had been fed meals by around thirty-five caterers but I had not been able to make my choice yet. But it was a nice learning curve and I was looking forward to the challenges it threw my way.

Midway into my assignment, Chirayu called and ruined my entire tempo and style of working. He complained he had been getting too many odd reimbursement requests from me lately, mostly food bills from places like Pune Bites, Pandey Ke Tunde and various others. I explained these food bills were part of my official assignment to judge potential caterers by the quality of their food so that I could make an informed decision. At this he blew his lid, as though I was buying my lunches off his fucking fixed deposits. He went off on a trip about how I was supposed to stick to the list of options the board had given me. I tried reasoning that my style of working was to step out of my boundaries and explore means to enhance customer delight. At this he started mouthing the kind of words only classless people like him had ever heard of. I can't replicate most of that conversation here. But the gist of the discussion went something like:

'You have to send every hotelier a valid quote request. If they invite you to a tasting session, they have to fill out a form with a registered stamp.'

'You have to be kidding me.'

'Without the stamp I am not reimbursing you a rupee.'

'You have to be kidding me.'

'I want an email copy of the quote request in the next hour.'

'You have to be kidding me.'

'And don't you dare forward your personal meal bills again. Do you think I am a chutiya?'

'...'

When things calmed down some days later, I slipped in the news of my week-long Switzerland junket to Chirayu.

His response was 'Let's see I can't promise anything right now.'

'But the airlines cannot block my tickets forever. I need to confirm my plan and also inform the organizers,' I explained what did not need an explanation.

'Let us see, we will take a call at the right time.'

Raghav sympathized with me. I met him over one of the weekends I was in Mumbai to file my documents for the Schengen visa. He told me to go right ahead and plan my Swiss trip without giving a flying deuce about Chirayu's caveats; he would manage the show in my absence. We then got crazily drunk and made jokes about Chirayu all night. He also thanked me for helping him with that financial loan.

'What would I do without your help?' he looked at me, teary-eyed, and just like that, the entire conversation became a little awkward and overly sentimental.

So I swiftly changed the topic and discussed updates on 'The Wedding Project'. He told me I had been doing a great job on-field on this project and that I should not give in to clerical pressures the senior management was subjecting me to. My heart ached to think I could not have Raghav as my manager instead of that other useless douche.

I did not meet Mehek on that visit. She had been terribly upset with me after all that had transpired in Mysore, and I was not keen to apologize either because, well, what else do you expect when you hand out half-baked information about your relatives? Anyway, when I returned to Pune, I called her and buried the hatchet by saying something nice and mushy. On her part, she promised me she would learn to tame her temper (Thank God for small mercies!); in fact, she said she had already enrolled for some evening meditation classes that apparently had the magic ability to transform stressed and aggressive people like her into peaceful zens. I thought that was a fantastic idea that would help us in the long run; she could take extra classes too if she thought they were any good. She then took undue advantage of my compassion and started demanding that I call her father and tell him about my selection at the symposium, and say something flattering about how his strict admonishments in the past had motivated me to work hard and achieve this feat. This ridiculous proposition sent our relationship into yet another round of turbulence until further notice.

Thankfully things were at least looking up on the project. Six of the eight vendors I had initially approached responded to my request for quotes. The sixth one did not have an internet setup at his facility, so I had telephoned him and had asked him to fax me his quote. The same evening I received a response from him that went:

Respected Sir,

Great news regarding your request for coats. My sister-in-law who runs a boutique in Chinchwad has agreed to co-operate in our business venture. She will design the coats for all the wedding guests at a discount of 20 per cent if ordered in bulk. The offer will also include mehendi designs and exotic lehengas for the ladies...

The remaining five guys were awesome. They not only sounded very receptive to pricing flexibility, but they also invited me to their dinner buffets almost every evening. I was so ecstatic and flummoxed all at once, I had to ask them to let me divide my time equally between them so no one would be disappointed. One of those evenings, Chirayu called again. In a 100 per cent concentrated sycophantic tone, he informed me that the prospective bridegroom Shri Haresh Patel had kindly shown personal interest in the preparation of the event and was flying to Pune the next morning to meet Karan, Arjun and me and to specify his preferences if any.

'I have also been considering your holiday request,' he added, 'and I don't foresee a major obstacle in my desire to approve it as long as you fulfil all preparations for the wedding and submit a consolidated cost report to Raghav before you leave.'

I had not seen a problem with this arrangement until Haresh Patel showed up and displayed what a project crisis can really mean. Arjun escorted Haresh to my hotel the next evening, carrying his travel trolley around for him. I met them in the lobby and was slightly surprised by how different Haresh looked to what I had imagined him in my head. He looked reasonably handsome although in an affected NRI-for-six-months way, spoke glibly, and had blue eyes which he insisted was his real eye colour although strangely neither of his parents had blue eyes. He had just returned after completing his MBA from Connecticut. I asked him why he went through the ordeal when he was already a millionaire, he gave me a very long and convoluted answer which I did not remember once our meeting ended—and he was now here to, in his words, 'thank you guys for your hard work'. He had already thanked Karan and Arjun in great detail, he now wanted to thank me over dinner before flying out of the city straight into an exotic spa that had offered to give him a Golden Glow massage—bridegroom package. He asked Arjun to hand the luggage to the driver who was assigned to drop him off at the airport.

At this, Arjun looked like the sky had fallen on him. 'Actually, Hareshji, if you don't mind, I would love to leverage a potential opportunity to pitch in to the role of your driver to n...'

'What?' Haresh asked incredulously.

'Can I drive you to the airport instead?' Arjun rephrased his question. 'I could use that drive as a good forum to present you with some interesting art concepts that can be succinctly translated into framed paintings in all the guest rooms...'

'Yeah, ok, ok, you can pick me up after dinner,' Haresh calmed him down.

'Great!' Arjun grinned victoriously. 'As per our discussion, I confirm I will pick you from The Great Punjab at nine. Please revert to me for any change in the schedule.'

Of course, Haresh did not bother to respond this time. I accompanied him to The Great Punjab, where I was very tempted to order some greasy gravies. But when he started dissecting his ordered plate of sautéed mushrooms and peas with a fork and a knife, I lost all interest in my order and began staring at his plate. Haresh had little value to add; he said I had already evidently put in a lot of effort behind the entire event and he would not want to interfere in my methods. That was all I needed to hear. Chirayu would now have no reason to reconsider my travel plans.

And just as we were preparing to leave, Haresh threw a spanner in the wheel with, 'Oh, all I must specify is that please ensure Clafouti is served at the dessert counter on one of the sangeet or the wedding evenings.'

Needless to say, I had never heard of the thing. So he

proceeded to give me an account of his travails to France and how he had so much wealth that he had no better idea than to squander it all away on every eatery that the country had to offer. The Clafouti stayed with him, and he now wanted to bring the French flavours alive at his wedding. Of course, this demand killed a part of me because I would now have this extra burden of overseeing the Clafouti deal with whichever vendor I finally chose. At that moment, though, I did not hear any alarm bells ringing, so I calmly accepted the demand.

Arjun arrived at the restaurant fifteen minutes ahead of time, palpitating furiously as he ran towards us.

'Where is your phone?' He yelled at me. 'I have been trying your number for ages!'

I felt my pockets; I must have left it in the hotel room. What was his problem anyway? Haresh looked at both of us, puzzled.

'The police are looking for you!' He said, his arms flapping in the wind like a pair of doves. 'Go back to the hotel immediately. Hareshji, please come. We must leave for the airport.'

What sort of cheap joke was that, I asked Arjun as he opened the passenger door of his second-hand non-sedan car to let Hareshji in. (Had he told me he was so desperate to drive Haresh to the airport, I could have considered lending him my Sonata).

'I am not joking!' His arms were about to fall off his body now. 'There is an entire gypsy of policemen outside the hotel, and some cops are making enquiries about you.'

He started the car, and with the windows rolled down he turned to Haresh and started lamenting the state of affairs in the country. 'No corner of this country is safe anymore, Hareshji.

You never know what's lurking in the dark alley. Anyway, let us go.'

Haresh looked at me sympathetically. Actually, he looked more worried about who would look after his Clafouti if something untoward were to happen to me. He pulled out a bottle of hair oil from his satchel and handed it to me.

'It relieves stress. Do try it,' he insisted. 'Rest assured, everything will be fine.'

I appreciated his faith in me, but I couldn't see how hair oil would help me escape the police for whatever reason they were after me in the first place. But I had to oblige, because the management would drown me in that very puddle of oil if they found out I had turned down the Lalwani son-in-law's gesture of generosity.

Arjun Bastard winked at me and then drove them off into the blindness of the night as I felt myself go weak in the knees. The police were looking for me? Was it the You Porn link I had accidentally opened on the hotel network while innocently trying to dodge various pop-ups on this online European travelogue I was going through? I did not think the cyber police was effective enough to track me down like that. I held a corner of the fence rail by the road side.

I felt faint.

8

The Name Is Rao—Bhaleshwar Rao

PHEW. I LIVED through that night to tell you my tale after all. On the upside, some fuck-ups in life do well to make you appreciate the simpler, duller days you should be grateful about. No, I am not talking about the police gypsy outside my hotel. I can talk about that later. I had a bigger crisis to deal with.

Haresh's Clafouti had become the death of me and potentially of my budding career as a Pulitzer prize-gobbler. With the deadline snapping at my heels, I now had a formidable situation: none of the shortlisted five vendors knew what Clafouti was. Four of them refused to add it to their menu. The fifth tried, and invited me as the guinea pig one evening. After eating a bowl I had to spend the rest of the day between the toilet and SOS Skype calls with Chirayu, Raghav, Bala, and the board of directors. Later that week, after having expanded my search options, I learnt that the luxury chain The Rembrandt, had an in-house chef who was half-French and could prepare Clafouti with his little finger. I was called for a tasting session, after which I had no reason to not believe their claim. The Rembrandt's management informed me they would be more than happy to take up the contract. Then their high-nosed in-command told me their only conditions were that any changes to the decided menu would incur a 2 per cent surcharge on the originally decided quote. And what was the quote? Nearly three times the average of the other five vendors.

'The situation is delicate,' I relayed to the board. Everyone on the other side of the video conference looked like they were going to cry. 'We cannot disappoint the girl's in-laws,' one of them said. 'Clafouti has to be included.'

Another argued that we could not overshoot cost projections under any circumstances. 'We might need to deploy the model of approximation on the Clafouti,' believe it or not, but this comment was made too. 'Ask the vendors what is the closest in taste and appearance to Clafouti that they can offer.'

'Meanwhile, Raghav, please send us a delta graph of the cost per head and the projected total cost differential if we go with The Rembrandt,' Bala ordered. 'Also please consider certain unknown variables in your calculations—such as the possibility that certain factions of the crowd may not eat a French dessert given their demographic profiles and religious inhibitions.'

Midway through this discussion, Raghav suffered a mental implosion at the hands of all these decision-makers. He asked everyone to shut up until I had spent some more time negotiating amicably with The Rembrandt—which I did once again at the cost of my dignity. The manager at the hotel stayed elusive for almost one lifetime, before his receptionist called me one afternoon and said he would now meet me. I met him—Karl, originally Koral Mehta—and explained to him this was no small contract and we were talking about Mr Dayanand Lalwani himself. He did not know who Dayanand Lalwani was. I explained he was the owner of Bytesphere. He said he did not know what Bytesphere was either. By now I wanted to slap him, but I somehow maintained my calm and negotiated additional services of spa treatments for the guests at their hotel if they agreed to get a little sensible about the price.

'*Pas un hasard*,' Karl responded with a twitch of the brow. 'Not a chance, in case you don't understand French.'

This man had too much attitude for someone who had taken fast-track French tuitions from somewhere near Garware Chowk. In my entire career I had not been spoken to in that manner by anyone except Chirayu, Anand Rai, Bala and the eight clients (and their respective receptionists) that I had worked with until then. I was done dealing with him. I sent another report to Raghav and the board with my two best recommendations: one, we stay within our stipulated costs and ask one of the five vendors to make Vanilla Soufflé and call it Clafouti; two, we go full throttle and get the Clafouti even if that means a truncation of our decided bonuses (how much more could the bastards truncate anyway, but I didn't include this in the report). This predicament was taken very seriously, as a result of which an urgent townhall meeting was summoned in the Mumbai office to discuss solutions. Bala asked me to relax and continue making smoother attempts at negotiating with *The Rembrandt* until the board came up with a plausible alternative.

With the board having responsibly taken this load off my

shoulders for whatever little time, I had some room to reflect over the surreal night gone by. So, when Arjun told me the police had been looking all over for me, my immediate desire was to run to the railway station, board whatever train came chugging along, and never be seen in the city again. Then I realized what a stupid proposition that was. So I ran back to the hotel and freaked out again on seeing, indeed, a police gypsy and a patrolling jeep lined up in the lobby, a constabulary of at least six policemen standing around them, looking very purposeful about their presence. I somehow gave them the slip and walked past the turnstile towards the reception desk. The hotel manager sat there looking very bored, examining his gelled hair in the gloss of his wooden desk. He looked like he had grown a wicker gate on his head. A sadistic smile appeared on his face when he saw me. He asked me to wait right there as he called a number and said, 'Sir, your man is here.'

Presently a well-built shadow emerged from the dimness of the waiting area towards me. It was the kind of scene that could remind you of Tom Cruise's famous walk in Top Gun with the crimson sunset in the background. Except when the shadow made itself entirely visible, I saw he was a hairier and stubbier version of Tom Cruise and there was absolutely no pleasantness on his face. He asked me for my mobile phone and a photo identification, skirting any nervous questions I tried asking him.

'First get me your phone please,' he said.

This process would have been a little less arduous had the entire population of the hotel not been watching the show. Why was it so difficult for people to mind their own business? As though I was bloody about to start a striptease. One elderly guest also accompanied me into the elevator as I went up to get my mobile phone and license, lamenting the hypothesis that my parents did not beat the shit out of me in my childhood because of which they would now have to see this shameful day. I asked him if he even knew why the police were here, to which he mumbled, 'Your generation something something,' and then thankfully left me alone at my floor.

By the time I returned downstairs with the belongings demanded of me, Tummy Cruise had been joined by his constabulary that was earlier hanging around in the porch, and they all looked impatient. Cruise examined my license, checked my last received calls (I think I had missed some twenty-two calls—this was a first; I had never received twenty-two calls in a single day) and then he reprimanded me for not taking calls that mattered. He looked at a constable and nodded tersely, at which the constable went for something that was lying in his hip pocket.

OH MY GOODNESS THEY WERE GOING TO SHOOT ME.

I closed my eyes and braced myself. This was a very poignant moment. I had heard a man's most significant landmarks flash before his eyes as his life draws to a close. Somehow all that flashed before my eyes was my first day at the Bytesphere orientation when I had asked my presenter if the company believed in an open-door policy, to which he replied, 'Of course, every time you see a superior around you, you open the door for him' and then everyone in the auditorium had laughed for nearly forever…

I opened my eyes when I heard a jarring commentary: 'PA

to Control Room... PA to Control Room, come in...'

The constable had a walkie-talkie glued to his ear. He responded with 'Target acquired, hello, target acquired, ROGER!' which was obviously his politest way of referring to me.

The walkie-talkie responded with, 'ROGER, relaying to Mysore Control room. Over and out.'

By now I had given up trying to comprehend what was going on. Tummy Cruise read my mind and smiled broadly, leading me to a couch in the waiting area. All of a sudden, the pissed-off expression in his face had given way to a warm, friendly glow.

'Mr Kapoor, it is so nice to meet you, let's get a drink and then talk,' he offered to my surprise.

Two lemonades were called for. He finally told me his name: Bhaleshwar Rao, Senior Police Inspector, Zone 3, Pune. I asked him the rhetorical 'How can I help you?' to which he began giving me a detailed account of how and why his team had come searching for me. He had only about finished detailing his family history when his phone rang.

'You can now hear the story from the horse's mouth,' he winked, and then spoke into the phone. 'Sir! Rao reporting, Sir...yes, Sir...I am right here with your son-in-law.'

He handed me the phone with a smile. 'Your father-in-law, the Police Commissioner of Mysore is on the line. He has been waiting to speak to you all day. He sent a search team when he could not get in touch with you.'

'Where have you been, beta!' Daddy Gupta cried out on the phone so convincingly even I nearly felt sorry for him. It was not long before I felt the urge to find out what had prompted the sudden outburst of love, but the mystery unfurled on its own.

He explained that Mehek had told him about my selection at the symposium, 'which is fine', he added casually, but he thought the book contract was something phenomenal, 'although I always knew you had some latent potential that was just waiting to be stoked by some motivational talking, beta.'

At this point I had got a sneaky feeling it may have been a little too early to talk about the book contract, but if that turned on the Gupta household, I was all for it. He then explained how worried he had been (and Mehek, apparently, was psyched out beyond repair—what was new about that?) when he had not been able to get through my number all day.

'After all, you are family now!' he declared, after which he started making remarks indirectly alluding to the thought of marriage, such as, 'By the way, are you really thirty? Do you know I was twenty-seven when we had Mehek?'

Fifteen minutes later, he suddenly remembered we were talking on Mr Rao's phone, who, as I could see, was getting increasingly fidgety.

'You carry on now,' Pop-in-law to-be said. 'Anyway now we will talk everyday to catch up. Do you have a webcam?'

'Uh…'

'My yahoo id is *supercopgupta*. I will add you so that we can chat comfortably. Do you have a Yahoo id?'

I had a Yahoo id which was created in 2004, and it was called *wellhung4u*, so I told him I did not have a Yahoo id. He insisted I got myself one. 'Or let it be,' he suggested, 'I will ask my secretary to make one for you.'

I started protesting that I did not wish to jeopardize national security by taking a city police chief's web time every day like that, but he would hear none of it and hurriedly hung up because he had to go cut a ribbon at a new cinema hall in the city. For any other problems during my stay, I could always get in touch with Mr Rao, he said.

Mr Rao nodded reiteratively as I handed him the phone screen. I convinced him I had no real need for any police protection or escort any place. I briefly told him about my skirmish with Karl from The Rembrandt and about the chip on his shoulder that was anyway not going to let me stay in the city for too long. I was still grateful for his offer of help, I said, and would let him know if I would need him for anything. And thus, our conversation that night ended after which I read something that made me so mad I could have killed someone and then met Rao again for entirely different reasons.

9

Number One Or Two?

THERE IS A reason I likened this company to a circus. There is a reason I felt a lack of strength of character here. For nowhere else in my life was I ever to see an Arnab Goswami to Simi Grewal type of transformation in a person at the speed of light.

Two emails from the management in the space of ten hours the next morning: the first one at 8.00 a.m. was titled 'Your Last Chance'. The second one at 6.00 p.m. was titled 'Are You Going Away With No Words of Farewell?' What had ensued between these ten hours was my entertainment and someone else's torment.

Were it anyone else in the situation, I would have felt compelled to feel sorry for the person. But because this was Chirayu, his sniffles felt like an empowering drug. I was so happy to see him squirm like a worm, I was almost sure I could die peacefully now. To think that I had waited for this moment since the time he had asked me to take his daughter's iPhone to a mobile repair shop in Kalyan just because that was the only shop that would give him a 50 per cent concession and because he could not go because his bullshit GPS did not recognize Kalyan on its map. This was almost three years ago.

Now, I had not just him but practically the whole of Bytesphere at my feet. All it took was my usual negotiating wizardry, Karl's hot-headedness, Chirayu's bad karma which he will never acknowledge, and someone's external support which I wish I would not have to acknowledge. But this followed some early bouts of nervousness and insane rage I was subjected to that morning.

Let us break this down.

What was the mission statement we were all trying to answer?

To get the son-in-law's Clafouti served at the wedding.

What was the problem statement?

The only caterer that knew how to make Clafouti was charging us a bomb.

What was the course of action decided?

Chirayu or Anand or Bala would return to us with a plausible solution.

What was the solution? This piece of pompousness that hit me early that morning:

From: Meenakshi Reddy (HRD)

Subject: Your Last Chance

Time: 8.01 a.m.

Dear Nakul,

On behalf of Chirayu and Anand, I am pleased to offer you a two-pronged strategy to combat the current situation. You can take either of these prongs and prick yourself with it. (This was not in the email, but was there in spirit).

1. *Take a risk-based approach: Retain the initially chosen vendor, ask him to make the best Clafouti possible. If the results are not satisfactory, we will reconvene after the wedding to discuss necessary proceedings that might have to be exercised against the responsible —including but not limited to degradation of roles and potential termination of services.*
2. *Take a client-driven approach: Play safe and pursue The Rembrandt. Feel free to use the Bytesphere model of Recycled Negotiation in tackling Karl. This Bytesphere model has a proven record of over 95 per cent success in our client and vendor engagements.*

Given the urgency of the matter, we would strongly recommend Option 2. Should the negotiations still fall off our planned track, this must not affect the project plan at any cost. In keeping with the Bytesphere spirit of placing company interests above personal interests, you might want to consider alternate ways to contain our budgets. We will adequately compensate you in return, but those modalities

> *can be discussed later.*
>
> *Also, your leave request for the end of this month has been declined in keeping with the company interests of a smoothly conducted wedding and given your inability to have closed the deal in the stipulated time. Once the wedding is successfully seen through, you may re-apply and we will reconsider.*
>
> *Regards,*
> *Meenakshi Reddy, HRD*

On a positive note, this turn of events had given me enough fodder to finish writing that book I had been pottering around with for very long now. Because no other source would be as inspiring as the idiocy the Bytesphere management had been inflicted with. On the downside, this practically meant I would not be able to make it to the symposium without rebelling against these morons by possibly putting in my papers.

Not surprisingly, Chirayu did not answer my calls when I tried questioning him about this what the fuckness. Raghav did answer, but his response was 'Do the right thing', for that was the best he could offer me—the company's budgets would not allow for him to travel to Pune and give me a helping hand. And the situation anyway looked like a deadlock.

'Threaten them,' Mehek offered a brilliant suggestion later that day. 'You don't *really* need to leave. Just *tell* them you are resigning. They will be forced to change tack.'

While I was reasonably confident about my importance in the company, I was not entirely sure the board would crumble under such pressure.

'What do you have to worry about anyway?' she then prodded me. 'You have another career waiting to take off...'

Of course! How had I not thought of this all along? And just like that, I found the key to putting every ass in the senior management in his right place—in a single word.

RESIGNATION.

'I am going to resign as soon as I hang up on this call!' I cried out excitedly.

She said she was very happy and excited about my decision and that she would stand with me through thick and thin at all times. Then after a pause, she did swing a little between 'You are sure you are getting that publishing contact, right?' and 'Never mind if push comes to shove I can provide for both of us.' Both the remarks unsettled me a good degree, but they were not enough to make me reconsider my decision. Some decisions were purely driven by fate. It was clearly my destiny that had landed me this horrible project, which in turn introduced me to Karl who turned out to be an A-level dickhead, which in turn drove me to the brink. The reassurance that $50,000 were just around the corner was just a coincidence. With that kind of frustration I would have chucked my job even if I were to have struggled my way through instead of being accorded this special treatment by Crown. And then, $50,000 were just the beginning. It gave me goose bumps to even imagine the change of fortune that lay ahead. Had JK Rowling even got $30,000 for her first contract? I did not know. And now she had created a kingdom of her own fantasies. DID JK ROWLING HAVE TO PLEAD WITH ANYONE FOR A HOLIDAY?

I needed to calm down. But I had developed wings. No, I

could not contain myself in my hotel room and cry like a sissy. I was liberated. I had a detailed breakfast in the lobby, burped with the kind of satisfaction I had not felt ever since I had come here, and then headed out with my laptop. The valet offered to get my car, but I opted for public transport for a change. I needed to get out of the comfort zone these leather interiors and fancy surround sound music systems I was getting used to. I wanted to be one with the commoners around me in order to understand what the consumer sought from his artist. I took a rickshaw ride to the nearest Café Coffee Day, ordered a caramel latte, logged into the company portal and first submitted my resignation. A field at the end of the form asked for my reason for leaving *in no more than eight hundred words*. I drafted a long paragraph detailing my experience and thanking my bosses, then I halted: wait, who was I kidding? Why was I being nice to these fellows? They did not deserve my politeness. They deserved to know the truth. And the truth did not need eight hundred words. Eight words would be just right.

I am fed up of all of you, I wrote, and submitted the resignation form.

Fifteen minutes later, Chirayu called asking me if I had spoken to Karl and that he hoped I had received his ultimatum. I said yes, I had, and I had left a surprise for him in his inbox as well, after which he would have more than just the ultimatum to be concerned about.

'What do you mean?' he asked, but I disconnected and switched off my phone.

Then I ordered another caramel latte and laughed to myself as I imagined Chirayu's reaction at the other end. Poor fellow would be left scrambling to get this Clafouti organized without my help. I felt sorry for Raghav, he would have to bear the brunt of my decision, but I trusted him to effectively manage this crisis. As I had nothing much to do before I packed and left this city to never return again, I spent some spare time reading about JK Rowling's inspiring success story. What a genius of a woman, rising in that manner, like a phoenix, from an impoverished mum to an I-have-never-seen-that-kind-of-money fortune. Being an author was the real shit, man. Anyone could be a top-notch corporate executive rolling in stocks and money like I had been all this while. But not everyone was a JK Rowling. I would need to be a little prudent with selling rights to these filmmakers, though. I had heard of some shady type producers who never credited writers for their work. Maybe if someone came up with a well-written set of clauses I would give it a fair thought. But I feared my stories would be turned into one of those commercial musical charades our films are known for, and then all the romance would be lo…

The staff asked me if I'd like some more coffee. I looked around. The café was teeming with customers; there were some who waited for tables to be freed for them. I saw them chatting away, idling away on their smartphones, with an evident lack of purpose in their lives, quietly floating away with time. I smiled to myself; I hoped they would all see a direction one day the way I had today. It was not so difficult, after all. I followed the waiter to the billing counter.

'Seventy-eight rupees,' he said. I fished for my credit card from my wallet.

'Minimum Rs 100 for the card, Sir,' he smiled.

I fumbled for cash, I did not have enough. He said there was an ATM right outside. I was just about to turn when I sensed a figure behind me at a good distance, moving towards me frantically. A big leap. I was grabbed by the arm. My wallet went flying in the air. It was caught by his outstretched hand. I turned around and met his gaze. A uniformed policeman. His smile was as terse as the shake of his head.

'You will not pay,' he instructed me as I saw the colour go off the cashier's face. The customers looked at me, as perplexed as I was. The constable then pulled out a hundred and handed it to the cashier, took the change and escorted me towards the exit. Outside, he introduced himself as a certain Mr Kamdar, smiled a little more willingly and explained he had strict instructions not to let me pay anything while in Pune. He had visited the hotel nearly at the moment I had left, and had followed my auto rickshaw all the way to Café Coffee Day.

'Whose instructions are these?' I asked.

'Rao Sir,' he said, and quivered a little at the mention. 'He will be looking after all your expenses here. You are our guest in the city.'

I was very touched and all that but was equally embarrassed. I explained this was absolutely unnecessary, but he stuck his tongue out in fear and said, 'Rao Sir will come to know, then...'

And so, the arrangements stayed.

I hailed an autorickshaw. 'Koregaon Park?'

'Two hundred and eighty rupees,' the driver said with a precision as though his brain had processed the proposed distance in the time he had rubbed his gums and released red spittle. Then Mr Kamdar peeped menacingly from behind my shoulder, and the driver instantly turned on the fare meter and let me in.

'Or we can go by the meter,' he said ponderously.

Mr Kamdar followed in another rickshaw; I intermittently looked behind to see his arms jutting out of his rickshaw to clear meddling traffic. I was very grateful but this needed to stop somehow. At the hotel lobby, I thanked Mr Kamdar profusely for his help and told him I was anyway leaving the city in the next hour or so, and then gave him details about my resignation and everything that had preceded it. He spoke very briefly to Mr Rao on the phone, nodded, and then said, 'You won't have to leave the city. Please take rest now and let me know when you step out again. Come, I will walk you to the lift.'

As we passed the reception, he asked me suspiciously if the food in the hotel was alright. The staff at the bell desk looked at me, annoyed, but what was I to do? I just meekly nodded and then ran for the elevator. Inside my room, a note was stuck on a decorated basket of Shrewsbury biscuits.

Dear Mr Kapoor, I visited your hotel this morning but you were not available. I would like to apologize for my ill-timed visit. Your phone seems to be switched off as well. Can you please call me at your convenience? This is about the catering contract. If you are willing to meet me, my car can come pick you up.

Regards,
Karl Mehta
The Rembrandt

Too little, too late. What was the point now? Chirayu was either minutes away from reading, or had already read, my ugly resignation form. And now the success of this otherwise impossible deal would get credited to him. I called Mr Rao. As I had suspected, he had had a chat with Karl. He said they went back a long way and that Karl would never refuse anything he asked for. In fact, he complained wistfully, had I met him a little earlier, he could have got the entire wedding organized for free. My head was spinning now. I tiredly ran him through the entire resignation story again.

'WHO IS THIS MANAGER OF YOURS?' He thundered.

I was very scared now. I calmed Rao down and explained it would be a breach of every corporate policy in the world if he participated in any official conversation with my management. Of course, if he had a plan to have Chirayu implicated in some scandal, I was game for a conversation, but I did not suggest such an idea myself. Rao cajoled me to reconsider my decision, otherwise both he and Karl would be extremely disappointed, and that I should at least meet Karl once. I reluctantly agreed and messaged Karl that I would come meet him in the evening. Karl was very excited and said a car would arrive at my hotel to pick me up. I indirectly had him cut out the flattery by telling him I had a car and he need not bother. He relented, and added that the hotel's Jaguar would just lie unused all day but that was ok. So I finally agreed to have the Jaguar sent to pick me up only because I did not want to sound arrogant.

Shortly after, Chirayu called and began abusing me like in the good old days when I used to consider such slander an assault on my dignity. Now I used his diatribe as a means of amusing myself or as a ray of hope that one day his anger would make him evaporate into a fat bubble that would eventually go poof. He challenged my resignation, said the words I had used in my resignation form were unprofessional and distasteful, and that he would provide a closing recommendation of never letting me rejoin the company in my lifetime. I said 'thanks' and hung up on him.

Stressed out of my wits, I changed into my tracks and set out to the neighbouring park for a run. Kamdar followed me and deposited himself comfortably outside the gate and had a long chat with the security guard about my relationship with the Police Commissioner of Mysore. I put on my headphones and ran for as long as I could, until I could take no more. All that circulation of blood pushed some to my bladder, so I headed to the pay-and-use toilet right in the centre of the park, where three patrons were already lined up to use the facility. Kamdar tiptoed behind me and gently prodded the queued patrons to step back. 'Urgent,' he said.

The coin collector looked at me in awe. 'Small job, one rupee. Big job, two.'

I dug my hands into my tracks, but Kamdar stopped me again and shook his head. Presently the toilet was vacated. I looked helplessly at the people who had been waiting before me. They were suitably pissed off already (no pun intended), so I just quietly went in and well, did my thing. When I came out, Kamdar made enquiries. 'Done?'

I nodded.

'Big job or small?' he asked. 'I need to pay this chap.'

I pretended I had not heard, put on my headphones and ran for my life towards the exit gate. Kamdar told me later he had paid Rs 2 at the toilet, hope that was alright?

I had an hour to kill before I was to leave for The Rembrandt. So I created a Yahoo id and chatted awhile with Mehek's father, who I will have to admit, looked much more intimidating in a police uniform. I asked him about the usual stress at work, to which he gave me a long account, interspersed with frequent admittance that he would be potentially overwhelming me with his achievements. I told him about Rao's persistence to have Kamdar pay for me wherever I went. He laughed heartily instead of agreeing to bring a stop to this. 'They like you,' he roared with laughter, 'that's all. Take Mr Rao along when you go to meet Karl. It will bring very positive results.'

I did not take Mr Rao along. But the results were very positive anyway. Karl was standing outside the gate of the hotel when his Jaguar drove me in. He hopped into the back seat and shook hands with me. It looked like he was almost about to embrace me but thankfully he noticed my unwillingness. I was spared the security checks and ushered past the lobby straight into the restaurant. 'Special guest,' Karl explained to the security. He then spent some time explaining how The Rembrandt stood out from other ordinary, run-down hotel brands because of its exquisiteness and exclusivity. Six-hundred rooms, three swimming pools, two gymnasiums, two massage parlours and four restaurants. Their food was never reused the next day. And if I looked around, he brought to my attention, patrons were even barred from entering the restaurants unless they were dressed in suitable evening attire. Suddenly we both glanced at my wrinkled t-shirt stained by Café Coffee Day's caramel latte. I reclined in my seat, looked out of the window and casually said that I hoped I would be excused because I had packed all other clothes as I was leaving the next morning. He frogged out of his seat and held me by the arm, telling me he would not let me go unless I handed the contract to him. To further enhance the deal, he promised me a 20 per cent discount on the overall package and additionally offered The Rembrandt's honeymoon suite free of cost to the married couple.

'Mr Rao and I go back a long way,' he reiterated.

I stopped Karl and ran him over the resignation story as well. At this rate, my resignation was not far from being national news. I told him about my face-off with Chirayu and his dirty threats.

'Come, let us teach him a lesson,' he said.

He led me to the hotel's internet centre and asked me to log into my company portal. I used my access code to get in, after which he gave me certain instructions, following which I sent this email to whomsoever it concerned.

To: Chirayu Chaudhary; Anand Rai; Raghav S

Subject: Clafouti –The Rembrandt

Hi, as you all may be aware by now, I have resigned from the company and would like to be relieved of all my responsibilities. But this is not without me fulfilling a promise—of having successfully negotiated with The Rembrandt on the catering deal. You will be happy to know that the cost is working out to Rs 40,000 less than what you had set me for. You can do whatever you please

with the money saved, I don't give a damn. Thank you for liberating me.
I will be leaving Pune tomorrow. You already have Karl's contact. I have already spoken to him and everything is sorted. Good luck with the wedding. Hope I get to see a video of Chirayu dancing at the wedding—just for laughs. So long, and thanks for all the fish. (Anand—wink.)

Regards,
Nakul Kapoor.

Karl patted me on the back, complimented me for the wonderfully caustic email and asked me to join him for dinner and watch the fun. Sure enough, an hour later as I was struggling to get through the platter of kebabs that had been thrust up my face from the buffet, Karl got a phone call. He flashed the screen before me and gave me a high-five, asking me if this was that dog of a manager. I nodded.

For the next ten minutes after he uttered 'Hello,' Karl stayed stoic and composed. The next words he spoke were, 'This offer does not hold good any more, I am sorry. I had offered this package because of Mr Nakul Kapoor, because of the professionalism and engaging purpose with which he conducted himself. Not like this, picking up the phone and giving orders…No, no, Mr Chaudhary, it serves no use if you come here and meet me now. I don't indulge in charity. This is business. That discount applied only if Mr Kapoor were to sign this contract with me. He informed me only this afternoon that he is leaving, and I am very disappointed. This has come as a shock to me after we had had all necessary discussions and promised all arrangements. He did tell me his decision was abrupt and was due to some differences with your company, but you know what? I don't care!...No, no, Mr Chaudhary, what do you mean you beg of me...even if you fall at my feet you won't get this deal with me now...no, no, Mr Chaudhary, that was just a proverb, you don't literally need to come to Pune and touch my feet, what nonsense...no, the answer is no. Either have Mr Kapoor visit me and sign the contract, or go look for another contractor. The Rembrandt always has plenty of options to stay in business anyway.'

Karl picked up a kebab skewer from our table and manoeuvred it with an evil twitch on his face. 'The chicken is walking towards the grill, Mr Kapoor. Tonight calls for a feast.'

Karl must have been an opportunistic twerp, but that night I let go of all my opinions. He almost felt like that superhero who had set the scene to bail me out. *In turbid times, when the chips are down... badamdash!...a saviour will rise unexpectedly and bring down an empire of bureaucracy... badamdash!...a new generation of heroes will be ushered... badamdash... !*

I had turned into a Karl Mehta fan by the time he came to the Jaguar to have me dropped back to my hotel. As per his instructions, I ignored Chirayu's calls for that night. The phone calls did not stop long after I had put myself to a very well-deserved sleep, but not before reading an email that had me laugh my guts out.

From: Chirayu Chaudhary

To: Nakul Kapoor; Anand Rai; Raghav S

Subject: Are you going away with no words of farewell?

Time: 11:23 p.m.
Are you going away with no word of farewell?
Will there be not a trace left behind?
We could have loved you better, didn't mean to be unkind,
You know that was the last thing on my mind!

Dear Nakul,

How are you? Let me first congratulate you on the adeptness you have shown in this project. It is simply exemplary. But on behalf of the company, I would like to express our sadness over your decision to leave us. As you know, we believe in retaining the best talent at all costs, and we will leave no stone unturned to make sure we understand your needs too. Please understand that any untoward conversation I had with you following your resignation was only because I was terribly upset and we did not want to lose you. Of course you can take leave! I extend my heartiest congratulations to you for your selection at the symposium, on behalf of all of us! You have added another feather in the Bytesphere cap with this feat.

I have mentored you under my leadership all these years, so I considered it my responsibility to ensure you always take the right decisions in a challenging situation. My exclusion from participating actively in this project was only to encourage

you to ramp up your consulting skills without my guidance. Now on seeing how easily you clinched the contract with The Rembrandt, I am proud to say that you have passed the litmus test. We do hope you will take this project to its logical closure and prove once again that the onus of a company's reputation rests on bright resources like you. Please reverse your decision to resign at the earliest. We are all here to listen to your concerns and act upon them. And then again, it has been so long since you have come home and had a drink with me, right? Are you free next weekend? Let us celebrate this wonderful achievement. I will cook pancakes too. Now please forget whatever transpired during the day and answer my call. Please.
Thanks Nakul. Once again, we are proud of you.

Chirayu

I would have replied, but…yawn. I turned off the lights and went to sleep, staring smugly at the star outside in the sky that shone on me.

10

Pain Tings

Now that Karl had gladly taken over the entire responsibility of all catering arrangements, I had time on hand to get done with that overdue manuscript. I spent the next seven days drinking caramel lattes in Café Coffee Day, sponsored by Mr Rao and Mr Kamdar, who always remained positioned within a radius small enough to gauge if I needed something. On the eighth day I complained to Mr Kamdar that the café was too noisy and I had been finding it difficult to concentrate. He was about to ask all the other customers to leave the café, but I told him I actually meant I needed to go someplace quieter. Within fifteen minutes, I was in the executive lounge of The Rembrandt, being offered piña colada and enchiladas. I asked Karl to relax and focus on getting the wedding food organized instead of pampering me. If I indeed had to check into his penthouse suite, what was wrong with my own hotel room? I only needed a quiet corner to write without being confined in the four walls of a room.

'Alright, but all your coffees are on me,' he declared.

'Ok, if you insist,' I said, but actually I had already assumed I would not need to pay.

On the tenth day, I organized what I had hoped would be my last web conference with Brian. The manuscript looked like a winner to me. It was an honest story about a young volcano of talent caught in a wrong job. It had all the elements Brian had asked for—humour and engagement with the reader which came naturally to me, and thrill which I added by getting the protagonist to bludgeon his boss to slow death in the darkness of his cabin at the end of the story. And while this was a story of an Indian software executive and not of The Wolf of Wall Street, I had also added unnecessary erotica just because Brian wanted it. And now the idiot was running all over my work by telling me it did not meet industry standards and that a lot of work was needed on semantics and structure. I told him I had spent adequate time already on it and did not think it needed to be tweaked any more, so he could either take it or leave it.

'Oh, in that case,' he said very dejectedly, 'I guess I will need to back out...'

I stopped him and asked him about our other options. 'The Augmented Package, $2000,' he replied cheerfully, wherein his team would work on refining my manuscript, would tune it to industry standards and voila! A bestseller would pop out and land in a publisher's lap. I had a sneaky feeling this was not likely to amount to much, but then he was the guy who had seen merit in me and it was in his own interest to ensure he knew what he was doing. Moreover I was not the kind of artist who believed in peddling his own work, and I would rather let it be picked by someone who already *wanted* to pick it. And then, $2000 was still loose change for me at the end of the day, especially considering the returns in store.

'Fine, just do your thing and let me know when you need me again,' I said and signed off before driving back to Mumbai.

Raghav insisted I lunch with him before flying out. Acknowledging his mentorship and support was in order, so I agreed immediately. I asked him if Karan and Arjun were joining us. He told me they had offered to stay back in Pune because relatives from both families were beginning to stream into the city the following week and they had volunteered to show them around the local markets and temples. Apparently the board was very touched by this gesture and had congratulated Karan and Arjun on this marvellous Masters in Sycophancy. But Raghav and I knew better, and were grateful the twosome would not join us for lunch after all. We had little bandwidth for people who had no real aspirations of their own.

When I reached Raghav's house, Billy Joel was singing somewhere in the backdrop of an intense aroma of Rajma-Chaval. Raghav stoned me with the food and then ensured I stayed stoned by offering me his bean bag. I handed him my pen drive with all the data on The Wedding Project and more particularly, the cost report. He felt a little guilty taking over from me after I had steered the company to safety and comfort already. Amused, I told him I hardly cared about getting credit for my work any more. I had already attained the self-actualization rung in Maslow's pyramid of human needs and did not view my peers as real competition any longer. But only to mitigate his sense of guilt, I was open to the idea of him putting in a letter of recommendation for me to the board of directors. He immediately skirted the topic and put on a Blu-Ray DVD of *Notting Hill* he had procured ages ago but had never found company to watch it with. I suddenly felt very awkward, slouching shamelessly like that in my superior's bean bag watching *Notting Hill* with him. I politely told him I needed to go home and pack, but he forcibly played the movie. By the time Grant and Julia had reunited, I was almost in tears, but not for the same reason as Raghav was. What was there in the film to get so soppy about? And which foolish heroine would fall for a local bookstore owner? It was not like he was a novelist, after all... After the movie ended, instead of letting me go, he asked me to fetch a surprise he had planned for me from the pocket of his trousers.

What is this yaar?

I mean, how do you draw the line between being nice and being assertive? I did not want any surprise. I did not want to put my hand in Raghav's pocket. I only wanted to spend the last few hours of that day with Mehek, because frankly now I was getting bored (though I didn't say that aloud). But he would hear none of it. So I reached for his pocket and plucked out two tickets to some French pianist's solo concert that evening at the NCPA.

Was he kidding me?

A musical concert that evening?

A pianist? A French one at that?

No matter how nice someone has been to you, sometimes you just have to put your foot down and learn to say 'no'. I said,

'No.' I did not want to hurt him, but I had really been bored out of my blood and bones when he dragged me along to that etymology seminar the last time I had driven down from Pune. So I affirmatively stood up this time, took leave of him very politely saying 'some other time' although I was pretty sure a piano concert would never happen in my lifetime.

By the time I had packed my bags and driven down to Mehek's, I had less than six hours to leave for the airport. There was no time to hold hands or to be compassionate or to discuss our future career plans. Practically speaking, we only had enough time to have sex and then sleep comfortably through the night in the softness of her water bed. But for some bizarre reason, she had just bought two ridiculously expensive paintings from an art gallery and now wanted me to help her nail them into the wall. I looked at her bewildered, as she uncovered two Chirayu-sized paintings and asked me to get started while she made us coffee.

I reluctantly held the paintings to the wall, had a closer look at them, and instantly got reminded of the paintings that had made me the first person in the history of my school to score a C- in Art. One was of a ship battling wreckage, and the other of a barren tree standing in the middle of a barren piece of land. She needed the first one framed in the living room, and the second one in her bedroom. So much for positive thinking. I got to work with some reluctance and swore to myself to reserve my opinions about her acquisitions, only she called out from inside the kitchen and asked me for feedback. I told her I did not want to comment, but she said my opinion mattered. So I told her I thought the paintings sucked and brought along a very negative atmosphere to an otherwise beautiful apartment. I also told her that since she had given me a lengthy commentary when I had bought myself a shirt worth $200 from Singapore on how I needed to be prudent with my expenses, I thought it well within my right to tell her that Rs 80,000 was not a sensible amount to expend on two nonsense paintings.

A huge fight ensued for the next hour or so, which finally ended with my saying, 'Actually this painting of the barren tree is very poignant. I think it symbolizes the firmness of hope against despair maybe I should buy one too.' Her face beamed with that explanation, after which we tried having sex very hurriedly. But I was so tired after nailing those paintings and fighting a lost argument that nothing, well, happened. I lay shamefacedly in bed next to her, staring vacantly at the barren tree hanging on the wall as I listlessly faced allegations that I did not find her attractive anymore and that maybe I was getting action elsewhere? Of whatever time was left, I slept like a baby on her water bed.

We drove towards the airport the next morning, making staccato conversation until she learnt I had gotten regular in my Skype conversations with her father. For some reason, this little detail overpowered her fear that I did not find her attractive any more. Anyway, I did not argue considering that at least she was in a good mood now and seemed to have called peace. Outside the airport, we stole time for a quick coffee, a less hurried kiss and a promise that this fondness for writing would turn out to be more than just a fleeting fad.

There was a long queue of travellers waiting to check in. A Jet executive saw me at a distance and waved me forward. Two minutes to check in, followed by a glass of Merlot at the executive lounge. Well, Bytesphere had come to some use after all with those frequent project travels!

At nearly one in the night, when I had boarded my aircraft, Raghav sent me a text: *Sorry to have bored you through the day. You should have simply told me you had to go meet Mehek, and I would not have insisted on the piano concert. Enjoy your trip.*

What had suddenly happened to him? Unnecessarily sensitive; I just did not know how to deal with such folks. I would chat with him at length once I was back. The aircraft was about to take off. And I had acquired wings now; there was no holding me back.

11

....

Kapoor's Angel

I WAS TAKEN by surprise when I stepped out of the airport in Zurich. Maybe I should have been better prepared. Brian had told me during a fleeting discussion that he had mentioned my name before Gabriel Jeffcott, the chief sponsor of the symposium, and that Jeffcott was extremely excited about having a near-about novelist be a participant at his event for the very first time. Brian had also told me that Jeffcott might want to meet me in person. But what was the need for him to come and pick me up at the airport? I had had six beers on the flight, had not brushed my teeth, nor had I done anything else that one must do before getting close to someone meeting you for the first time.

But there was no backing out now. Gabriel Jeffcott stood right in front of me, holding a placard in my name. He was dressed sharply in a double-breasted suit of metallic grey, a Harrods handkerchief peeping out of his chest pocket, a Movado watch glistening on his pink wrist.

I strode up to him and shook hands. 'Pleasure to meet you, Mr Jeffcott.'

'The pleasure is all mine,' the man replied. 'But I am Ali, Mr Jeffcott's chauffer. Let me get your bags.'

I was mindblown already. Once on the road, I casually asked Ali if the Movado was an original. He did not speak to me for most of the remaining journey until I realized he had been driving me around since the time his car had been manufactured and had to ask him where exactly he was taking me. He told me that my bed-and-breakfast was another thirty minutes away nestled in beautiful countryside, which I later found out was almost situated in fucking Germany.

I resented this a little, but Ali explained that Jeffcott had things arranged thus—he reckoned writers should be 'committed to an environment of recluse' so they could indulge their creative senses undisturbed. I was not sure why Jeffcott had such weird notions about creative indulgence. Anyway, I would talk to him about putting me up at the Baur Au Lac from the next night on, where the actual event was to be held. That was the least he could do for a privileged participant he had been looking forward to meeting.

An eternity later, we reached my lodge. After getting my luggage out of the boot and quickly posing for a picture with the Bentley, I asked Ali what time he would arrive to pick me up for the conference in the morning. Asking me if I had missed reading the conference rules, he flicked a brochure at me: except for the airport transfers, participants had to make all travel arrangements by themselves. Dejected, I asked Ali of my options. He reckoned it would be a very exciting experience for me to hire a bicycle from the bed-and-breakfast and ride down to the hotel so that I could soak in the beautiful sunshine. I read his expressions carefully to note for any signs of laughter. None emerged. I asked him to give me a more realistic option, such as how much would a taxi cost me to get there. He laughed this time, asked me to look around myself and wonder if taxies would bother plying around in such a region. There was no answer required: to the left and to the right of the road lay sprawling meadows till as far as I could see. Around two hundred cows lay scattered on each side. In the middle of it all stood my accommodation: Sunrise Bed-&-Breakfast.

'You can take a bus ride if you like,' he offered. 'There is one that leaves at 6.20 in the morning. The next one leaves at 9.05, but that might mean you will be late to the event. Having said that, Mr Jeffcott does believe a nice bicycle ride early in the morning does wonders to the thinking mind.'

One thing was certain. Gabriel Jeffcott was a psycho. I was not so sure I wanted to meet him anymore. Right then, I was too exhausted to do anything about the ordeal, so I just trudged up the stairway to…heaven. Wait.

WHAT WAS CAMERON DIAZ DOING AT THE RECEPTION DESK OF SUNRISE BED-&-BREAKFAST? I inched closer. She was on the phone, speaking a language I could not comprehend. Then she looked up at me with her blue eyes. Good God! I froze. She was not Cameron Diaz, yet quite nearly a spitting image of her—only younger, prettier and most definitely friendlier than Cameron would have been were she to check me in.

She introduced herself with a warm grin. 'I am Tamara, and you must be checking in?' Such a hot name, for a moment, I forgot my own name. She thought I had difficulty understanding her accent, so she started gesticulating. I blurted out my name. She repeated it in her soft, German-Belgian-French whatever accent. Full sweetness only. Unfortunately I was still very conscious of the six beers I had had on the flight through the night, so I stood a good distance away from her as I spoke. But she told me she was in the house almost all day and that I could holler any time I wanted. Of course I would holler! I sensed an instant connection with her. We chatted as though we knew each other for ages even as she had me fill out a check-in form. She then showed me to my room, suggested I get some rest because I looked very tired, and then when I woke up she could recommend some places I could visit. I mildly suggested that some company would do me wonders because sight-seeing was more fun in twos, so if she knew someone who would be willing to accompany me... She suggested I look up traveller forums online because a lot of backpackers often came to Zurich and were always on the lookout for company. Tamara was so innocent. A piece of purity. I needed to protect her from this cruel, scheming, voyeuristic world.

I took a long shower and flopped back on my bed for a couple of hours, dreaming happy thoughts about my future that was about to unfold. I also dreamt about Mehek. Then for a while I woke up, wondering to myself that in a hypothetical situation where Tamara fell head over heels in love with me and refused to let me go back to India, what would happen to Mehek? Would she want to let go? Would it be fair on my part to let go, myself? Would I feel torn between two very beautiful women or would I emerge a moral victor who would make a good, informed decision? I was too tired to think, so I put myself to sleep again. I did not wake up again that day.

12

Do My Calf Muscles Look Sexier Now?

SHE SMELLED LIKE daffodils. When Tamara got me breakfast the next morning—hash browns and something, does not matter—I noted she was a visual phenomenon in the mornings. Her blue pinafore belied the slenderness of her waist. Her ivory neck turned a shade crimson as we exposed ourselves to the glistening sun in her porch. But her smile was brighter. I skirted my gaze, but her nimble fingers were a regular distraction. Her lips moved like a song, and then she suddenly stopped talking and asked me if I was checking her out.

Embarrassed, I stuttered, 'No! I was only secretly admiring your impeccably fit body.' She laughed; it was the cycling, had I seen how toned her calves were? She put her right leg up, brought my hand to her calf. A perfect curve here too. Sensing the trepidation in my trembling fingers, she asked me if I would like to spend some time exploring her curves. Before I could react, she pinned me down on the table top. The cutlery went crashing to the floor. She drew a bread knife out of the Nutella jar and smeared a layer on my mouth, bringing her tongue down on me. Staring was impolite, but I could not stop looking at her as she brought her face towards mine. Daffodils. Nutella. A heady mix of the two fragrances, and we united…

… 'Will the bread be brown or white?' I woke up and peeped through the kitchen door. Tamara was frying an egg for me. How nice. But there was so much more to life than cooking and eating, yaar. When she finally sat next to me, nothing happened between us, but not because it could not have happened. In fact I am pretty sure there was potential for a great scene to build up, but she asked me if I had 'family'. I guiltily blurted out everything about Mehek, but made sure to add that both of us had been reconsidering the longevity of our relationship of late, and that sometimes I felt so lonely I wanted to cry and find comfort in a warm embrace. Tamara did not pick up that cue, but she did offer to ride along with me to the symposium in case I needed help with directions.

At this point all I could see was that it would be inappropriate of me to turn down my hostess' gesture of hospitality. Also, I had already missed the only bus that could have gotten me there and it was not like a limousine was waiting to ferry me across. What choice did I have?

We walked to the nearest public bicycle stand, during which time I quickly Googled 'Overcoming mental blocks to cycling' and realized it was not SUCH a big deal also. The link I hit on insisted that the human body was naturally built to sustain long periods of endurance; moreover cycling involved one of the most natural movements of the body that did not qualify as a threat to human health at all.

With this first stage of fear overcome, there were some easy tips provided to combat any genuine physical stress: break your journey into equal parts of convenient duration. For example, if you have to cycle 100 kilometres, look at it as twenty-five challenges of cycling 4 kilometres each. Not only does that break your stress, it also gives you twenty-five chances to feel proud of yourself and maybe, treat yourself to a small snack after every milestone (or alternately engage in a delectable conversation with your cycling partner).

Our journey was all of 9 kilometres. Easy-peasy. I mentally broke it into three instalments of 3 kilometres each and suddenly felt very upbeat about this entire pedalling business.

We picked up the bicycles. I watched Tamara set herself up as I did a light warm-up, which is the athletically correct thing to do before strenuous exercise. She was so nimble. She floated on to her bike and sped off, cajoling me to 'catch up'. This was naughty, stoking the alpha male inside me. I put in all my energy, pedalled at twice her speed and caught up with her in no time. The first three kilometres were a breeze. She complimented me upon my agility. She also added that I did not look like I would be this agile. I gave her the benefit of doubt, maybe she just could not express all that she felt because she was so obviously overwhelmed by what she saw.

From the fourth kilometre onward, I started feeling a mild tingle in my thighs. But that was exactly what the article had predicted! This was only my body's way of telling me I was doing great and that it was just toning up thanks to all that blood being pumped around. No pain, no gain.

So I sang the *Jo Jeeta Wohi Sikandar* song in my head and continued pedalling with ferocity. After the fifth kilometre Tamara asked me if I would like to take a short break, because I was turning crimson and she was worried that I was probably not used to so much physical activity and something bad was about to happen to me. Frankly, I felt a little offended by the remark; what did she mean I was not used to phy…I pedalled harder. By the sixth kilometre I realized she was probably right. I sensed the queasiness the write-up spoke about. Those waffles, so wonderful at breakfast, did not taste so great now that they were resurfacing and clogging my windpipe.

My Googled article cautioned readers against potential conditions of nausea and motion sickness, to combat which one was advised to fix one's gaze at a stationary object. I fixed my gaze upon the lovely Swiss Alps, which looked dependable. The trick seemed to work until the Alps began to sway a little dangerously. I faintly heard: 'Are…you…do you need…listen I can…medical…' but I did not stop pedalling till we reached the Baur Au Lac. Because my hands were now numb, I was not able to apply the brakes. So I allowed myself to do a free fall on to the garden overlooking the hotel.

Tamara dropped her bicycle and came running to ask me if I was alright. I shut my eyes and smiled, saying I was perfectly fine but I could not resist the softness of the grass and so I had let my cycle glide perfectly down on the ground; it was an old habit I loved following. I told her she could lie down next to me and soak in the serenity, but she said she was running late for some urgent errands. Once she was out of sight I opened my eyes, carefully flipped my body over and lay on my belly measuring the shortest distance to the lobby and began crawling across the garden diagonally. Twenty minutes later, I reached the doorway of lobby and was courteously hauled up by a very shocked valet. Breathing heavily, I held out my invitation card to the symposium. He put my arm around his shoulder where it flapped helplessly. I asked to be taken to the washroom, where my breakfast and I parted company over a sink.

With all due respect, FUCK GABRIEL JEFFCOTT AND HIS RULES. I was not riding a bicycle in my life again. I felt better fifteen minutes later, when Brian walked into the men's room and, after exchanging pleasantries, informed me that his team had nearly finished working on my manuscript and were about to start pitching it to a few publishers in New York even as I peacefully attended the symposium. I was willing to jump in excitement but only managed to stare at him vacantly with my mud-and-grass-smeared sweaty face and asked him to assume this was my happy expression. He got me to clean up some more and then took me straight into the ballroom that was thronged by all the participants, most of whom were dressed as though they were getting married.

Why the hell were they in tuxedos? I quickly rolled up the sleeves of my shirt to conceal its ripped ends, thanks to my misadventure with the garden and the road to the lobby.

Gabriel Jeffcott stood near the registration desk looking pink. He turned an elegant deep rose pink when he was introduced to me by Brian, I don't think he had been expecting me to land up. But Gabriel got a lot friendlier when Brian told him I was the novelist he had spoken to him about.

We chatted for a while, during which Gabriel told me

about the only book he had ever written. He pulled out a thick, battered book from inside his coat pocket: *The Tallest Elf*, by Gabriel Jeffcott. First print, October 1973. A very Plain Jane cover that solely depicted a goblin's hat, and a much younger Gabriel Jeffcotton on the back cover. 'A worldwide bestseller,' said a subtle subtext in white ink at the bottom. I took the safe cue and exclaimed I had heard so much about this book because so many wonderful things had been said about it; I had started reading it long back but had not got a chance to finish readi…

'Bollocks!' exclaimed Jeffcott, moving closer to me. 'Bollocks, you started reading it. Unless, of course, you started reading books when you were still in your diapers.' He caressed the cover of *The Tallest Elf*. 'The autumn of 1984; it was the last time my baby ever saw the light of day. No more prints were published since. It's like I scored an ace and then called it a day.'

'What happened?' I asked.

He grimaced a little. 'Complacency. My art did not change with changing times. The more "contextual" literature took over, and I did not find room in the crowd.' He looked out the window, biting his beard contemplatively. 'I first lost my position in the market, then I lost my confidence. Before I knew it, I had lost my intent.'

This gentleman was not giving me any confidence at all. First, he talked at length about his literary failures. On top of that, he explained how he was born rich and stayed stinking rich because of his businesses in hospitality and how he did not really need to bother about minting money by writing books. His last remaining connection with literature was the annual symposium he organized here.' Because writers may come and go, but the art must always live on,' he smiled sagely. 'Will you be the one I will be proud of, Mr Kapoor?'

Of course he would be, I shook hands with him reassuringly. And then seizing the right opportunity I subtly asked him if he could have me shifted to the Baur Au Lac itself, so that after the event maybe we could meet up for cocktails in the Executive Lounge and share our experiences of writing, etcetera or whatever suited him, as long as I could be spared that awful bicycle ride the next day. He waved at someone in the crowd, excused himself and told me he'd be back with me in a jiffy. That was the last I saw of him.

Minutes later a young fellow, probably a university student, ushered everyone through the doors. Brian was carried along by a wave of participants flocking around him, possibly trying to negotiate a publishing contract with him. Poor fellows.

When the day's interactive events started, I realized there was more than just my worn-out appearance that made me feel like a misfit in the room. Every participant out here looked like a superlative wordsmith to me. They were all married to literature, spewed Shakespeare and Rumi in ordinary conversations and forced me to covertly refer to my Wikipedia app for every book or author they quoted.

I had never run after books. This profession had found me. There I was, smug and happy in my utterly comfortable and rewarding job, where I had smoothly sailed past my peers to the enviable designation of ACNE. Everyone aspired to having ARRIVED. I was one of the few who actually had. But I accepted my unprecedented success graciously and humbly, conceding there might have been some merit in me that my company viewed as indispensable. But now, this book contract from Brian had me thinking again. Was I thrilled about it? Sure, I was delirious with joy. But this did not curb the inexplicable sense of being undeserving. Especially when I got to know my colleagues at the symposium better. Shivang Apte, the only other Indian in the group, had given up his job as a professor of English at Pune University over three years ago so he could focus on getting his first novel published. Almost every participant was a struggling artist, but me. Specks in a heap of dust, but me. Bricks in the large wall, possibly me too. But the fire still raged within them. Was I an exceptional talent, or was I just getting too lucky in life once again?

For now, the least I could do was to contain my ecstasy and to try and blend in with the other ordinary participants. There was no point waving the flag of your success before the less fortunate replete with unrequited dreams. Shivang asked me if I would be interested in exploring Zurich and then dinner that evening. I gladly obliged. I liked Shivang. He was a sincere professional and there was much to learn from him. And honestly, I couldn't help but feel sorry for him. I had been watching him frequently in conversation with Brian too, and while I was sure he had the ability to make a lasting impression with his knowledge of literature, it simply broke me to see that his dream was being run over by the very guy he wanted to explore the city with. I guessed I had no option but to gently break the news of my deal with Brian.

Which I did, when we ate dinner at Tastes of India in the city square later that evening. The food was a welcome change after the fist-sized chicken and carrot sticks we were offered for lunch at the symposium. Shivang seemed remarkably happy that evening and frequently spoke about how fruitful his attendance at the symposium had been for him and how meeting such accomplished people at the event offered him a renewed gush of energy after a three-year-long struggle to get his work recognized. I waited patiently before bursting his bubble by telling him everything. An awkward silence later, he congratulated me and said he was very happy for me. But I could see the dejection right through his veneer. There was very little I could do for him at that stage, but I could at least insist on footing the bill, no? He protested a little. But I told him it had been a while since I had utilized some of the silver points on my Mastercard and that he must allow me the privilege. He smiled gratefully.

I also offered him a ride back to his motel in the limousine I had hired from an agency. There was no way in the world I was bicycling my way back to Tamara's after what I had to go through that morning. When else would all my accrued (and the to-be-accrued) wealth come to good use? Yes, the limo had a steep rental, but I did not see any sense in being stingy when it came to considering my own well-being. And yes, Shivang's motel was a little off-route for which the chauffer mentioned an additional surcharge of 45 francs. Big deal! Would that matter to me one year from now? Probably not. But a good deed done for a good guy would stay with me always. Shivang could not stop thanking me for the gesture. Shortly before we arrived at his motel, he hesitantly asked me if I could put in a word for him with Brian.

'Just trying my luck,' he said a little sadly.

If it were anyone else, I would have dismissed the request

instantly. Publishing contracts were not won by earning favours, for God's sake. But I could definitely bend the rules for Shivang. He deserved a fair chance.

'I will speak to Brian when I get a chance,' I promised him, although I was very doubtful how much that could really help.

He smiled broadly, thanked me again, and walked away from the aura of grandeur that surrounded me. I felt relieved. This grandeur was scaring me already, I did not want to intimidate him with it. The limo turned around and drove me away. I looked out of the window, closed my eyes and surrendered myself to the burden of this new image I was about to create of myself.

13

Professional Colours

CHIRAYU WALKED OVER to my cubicle, knocked softly on my desk and asked me if I had a minute.

Wait. Let me recapture the moment.

He knocked softly. And then he *asked me for my time*. I was almost tempted to stand up, shake hands with him and congratulate him for finally having acquired some manners. The threat of my resignation had worked its effect longer than I intended it to. I was now beginning to feel a little sorry for him. But he was the kind of person who learned his lessons the hard way. So I simply stayed put and swivelled comfortably in my chair, offered him a disgruntled look and said we would need to make it quick because I was packing up early for the day.

He looked at his watch very sadly. I expected him to draw me a graph correlating extended work hours with individual growth. But he simply said 'ok' and then added he only wanted to let me know my appraisal rating was ready and if we could discuss and agree upon it, he could get it signed off for closure. To be honest, I was entirely free that day and had little on my agenda. But for one, I had to get even with him for all those times he had made me wait for ridiculous things like signing off on my travel reimbursements or my leave requests and for being a prick in general. Secondly, I considered appraisal discussions a waste of my time. I had been scoring a '1' so consistently that I would not be surprised if my peers' managers had even stopped fighting for their subordinates to out-compete me in the relative ranking. I opened my calendar, pored over it meaningfully and then looked at Chirayu and shook my head regrettably.

'Only after I return from Pune,' I said.

Poor chap. He looked like someone had stolen the whiteboard from his cabin. He said we were already past the deadline and HR had been hounding him to close all appraisals and it would be great if I could cooperate. I reminded him that closing appraisals wasn't my responsibility and I needed more notice to make myself available.

'I had called you often while you were in Zuri....'

'On official holiday,' I sighed and shook my head again. When would the wretch understand it was impolite to call people when they were on leave.

'I am afraid you will need to request HR for an extension,' I said.

He then asked me when I intended to leave for Pune. He spoke some very long sentence about how Karan and Arjun had exceeded the company's expectations by overstaying in Pune and ensuring they were around for any on-field requirements that would need to be tended to. I did not believe those guys would stoop to such levels to lick ass until I saw Karan's Facebook picture of him grinning from under a sleeping bag on the wedding lawns. Raghav was tagged in the picture, and the caption read: 'When work transcends your realm of duties and becomes your passion, your *raison d'etre*.'

I told Chirayu I had done what I needed to do as part of my responsibilities and I did not intend to get there until the evening of the wedding itself; hope that was alright. He sheepishly smiled and began walking back to his cabin. I called out and told him I almost forgot to add—I hereon needed a lot more time to concentrate on promoting my debut novel and I could not to do that staying in office all day long. So I needed the company to arrange an option where I could work flexible hours during the week. Chirayu said we would need to discuss this during my appraisal session. By all means, I shrugged, though this was hardly negotiable. Once he left, Gaurav Sonawane from the adjacent cubicle, whom I had never spoken to so far, came up to me and said he was very impressed with the manner in which I controlled my manager and that he would love to learn from me.

'Just good timing and some guts,' I winked.

I looked at Karan's picture again and laughed to myself. Because he had not got any likes that far, I decided to oblige him and to humour myself. I changed my profile name to 'Nobody' and then hit the 'Like' button.

I called Raghav later that evening just to check on him and to ask him if he needed me to come over any earlier to Pune. He seemed to have gotten over my polite decline of the invite to the piano concert. Thank God for that. He said everything was under control and he had been in constant touch with Karl.

'What about the cost report I sent you?' I asked.

Very uncharacteristically, he beat around the bush in response and said that except some formatting issues and a 'lack of professional colours in the bar graphs', all was by and large good and he had the report under control as well. That was a little unsettling, coming from a man who was known to despise conventional protocol and powerpoint presentations. Maybe it was just the stress leading to the main event.

Gaurav Sonawane called me the day I was on the road to Pune. He said his boss had asked him to stay back late the previous night and prepare a sales pitch on his behalf, in response to which Gaurav had apparently screamed 'Oh, fuck off!' If this was indeed and regrettably true I told Gaurav, it was not necessarily a wise and brave move on his part. But now that he had said what he had to say, I added, he could just take it easy and watch what happened next. His enthusiasm died a premature death on hearing my response; he said he was just trying to follow my footsteps of taking on anyone who tried to thumb him down. I said that was the right thing to do provided one was sure one had the standing and security to take such irreparable risks, as was my case. He suddenly went all frantic and frenzied, asking me if he should call his boss back and apologize to him because he hadn't heard back from him after the incident and maybe something was very wrong. I told him to sit back and relax now that it was all over, and I would mentor him nicely once I was back in Mumbai.

At that point in time I was pretty excited about seeing the output of all my dogged efforts at the Lalwani wedding. Not less than three thousand guests had thronged the Regal Lawns in Pune. Soft instrumental Garba music played in the background. Sixteen stalls, organized in a semi-circle along the perimeter, served food and wine. I took a deep breath as I looked around, proud of a job well done. Karl hadn't made it to the wedding himself, but he spoke to me on the phone and assured me he had stayed in constant touch with Raghav in my absence and the show was being managed just fine. Nonetheless, I took a stroll around the food stalls and made enquiries with the staff to ensure there were no possible lapses in store. The staff were a little perplexed to see me but only until I told them who I was. Then as part of my duty and commitment towards the project I randomly picked some dishes and tasted them to ensure dinner was going to be served nice and hot to the guests. The Clafouti lay in a corner in all its splendour, so I also dug a little into it to see what the fuss was all about. Nonsense. I could not believe this was what Haresh made me scurry around like a fool for. I had to consume another tikki chat to get over that insipidity. Meanwhile a grumpy relative from the boy's side came running from across the length of the lawn, demanding from the waiters who was trying to consume all the food before the groom and his family got to lay their hands on it. I first contemplated introducing myself. But then he did not look like he would be willing to exchange introductions, so I quietly slipped away and blended smoothly into the crowd before he saw me again.

During this time I was also conscious I was the only person strolling around the lawns all by myself, so I started searching some familiar faces. Minutes later, I saw Dayanand Lalwani chaperoning high-profile guests who were streaming in by the minute. The board of directors were chaperoning Lalwani in turn. And, guess who was chaperoning the board? Exactly—Karan and Arjun. I followed this swarm of black and grey suits as it snaked its way through the crowd and stopped near the stage where the wedded couple stood with fixed smiles plastered on their faces. Haresh noticed me through the flower boutique swinging before his eyes. We waved at each other. I gestured I would be with him very soon. I first needed to see Raghav and let him know I was back in action and happy to help around. I nudged Karan and Arjun inquiring after Raghav. They looked somewhat startled to see me, then smiled their fake smiles and shrugged cluelessly. Then they turned back and started talking to the directors, who weren't listening because they were talking to Lalwani, who wasn't listening because he was talking to his guests.

I could not stand the presence of this collective attention deficit disorder, so I quietly walked up the stage, congratulated the wedded couple, and had a brief friendly chat with Haresh. He asked me if I had been using his hair oil at all. I took a second to recall what he was talking about, and then said yes, of course, was it not showing in what a sprightly, stress-free person I had turned into since he had last seen me? Meanwhile, I had also finally spotted Raghav—looking in command of things as always as he interacted with some guests, blending in perfectly like a member of the host family. I excused myself and promised Haresh I would talk to him at leisure again. I went to Raghav and patted his back. He turned around, and like Karan and Arjun, was equally surprised to see me. 'Because you did not inform us you would make it!' he said. But obviously I would, I said, and then asked him if I could be of any assistance now that I was back to take some load off his shoulders. 'Sure, let me see, but I will be right back,' he said, and then sauntered away someplace I could not find him.

Shortly, the instrumental Garba music stopped. A jarring sound emerged from the microphone. A large number of guests turned towards the stage, where Dayanand Lalwani stood next to a—in the holy name of Christ—PROJECTOR! This company really knew how to take inanity to the next level. Nonchalantly, Lalwani began talking about how proud he was of the way the wedding had been organized by his company's trusted lieutenants and why he thought it imperative to acknowledge and reward their hard work on that very stage.

I don't know if the wedded couple had been consulted before this nonsensical ceremony was planned, but they both looked utterly helpless and distraught on seeing what was going on. I turned red with embarrassment myself. What was the need to create a scene here yaar? I mean, come on, this was not the first time we were getting an award (well I don't know about Karan and Arjun, but I could at least speak for myself). But this could have been accommodated in a more modest setup after we returned to Bytesphere, in front of all the other employees instead of bugging those poor unsuspecting guests out of their wits.

You should have seen how Karan and Arjun started prancing in front of everyone on hearing the announcement. Utterly immature and childish; I felt ashamed to note they were my peers at work. Given a choice, I'd have allowed one of the idiots to collect the award on my behalf also—they could have posed with it for all I cared. But I did not want to come across as being arrogant about my role in the project. So I reluctantly trudged towards the stage and stood behind Karan and Arjun, who looked ready to leap on to the stage any time. Bala appeared on the stage with the board of directors as they joined Lalwani and posed for a picture before the cameramen. I stood wondering what they were wait...good grief. One of them brought the projector to life and on it emerged, much to everyone's disbelief, the title 'The Wedding Project—Leveraging Resource Capabilities'. The entire gathering looked stunned. Small children, naturally more upset than adults at having their evening trashed, started crying. The adults looked at each other, confused. Some sniggered and those who knew Lalwani personally, avoided meeting his eyes.

Bala began speaking, 'Let us take you through a little journey of how our atomic level productivity...' when thankfully Lalwani looked at him and lip-synced to what I am pretty sure was '*Saalo, gadhedo!*' Bala nervously gestured to the technicians to turn the projector off and continued, 'In the interest of time, I will now directly call out the names of the core team that made this wedding such a grand phenomenon...'

Karan, Arjun and Raghav got on to the stage. I followed suit. We waited at a corner for us to be called forward as the cameramen got down to work.

'Karan for handling the entire logistics of the venue as well as these wonderful decorations.' Karan stepped forward and then refused to step back till every photographer had clicked his picture from every angle.

'Arjun for single-handedly managing the guests' accommodation and for ensuring local conveyance and entertainment on the days leading up to the wedding. I am sure he made you all very comfortable.' Arjun went up and accepted his reward. The fucker also waved at the crowd as though he were getting a bloody *Filmfare* award. By now the guests were beyond all levels of perplexity and frustration. I could not blame them. Surely not a soul in the crowd would have ever seen a prize distribution ceremony conducted during a wedding reception.

I would keep my presence short-lived in the interest of everyone's sanity. I inched forward in anticipation of the next announcement. I turned to Raghav to smile, but he had not seemed to noti…'And finally, Raghav for orchestrating the catering department and also for anchoring the entire event so smoothly.'

A large sense of vacuum. My ears droned with pain. I called out to Raghav to remind him I was yet to be acknowledged. But he stepped forward and joined Karan and Arjun. All three of them stood grinning ear to ear for the shutterbugs, the board and Lalwani standing around them. I tapped Raghav angrily. He did not even turn around to glance. I turned behind to look at Haresh who returned my look of confusion. The photographer stared at me irately and then asked me to get out of the frame; I would need to get into the line if I had to come pose with the couple later…

It took me a while to completely register what had just happened. This was not the first time someone in the company had turned out to be a prick. But the difference was I could usually identify a prick the moment I saw one. I had almost made the slimeball a role model!

I waited for them to get off the stage after which I confronted him and asked him if he thought the directors had forgotten to call out a certain name. He shrugged in response. 'You are free to go ask them. But if I were you, I'd have seen the project through to its closure before running off on leave. Food for thought, Nakul—there is a difference between getting into a boat, and steering it to the shore.'

A burning fever and itch overpowered my body as red rashes formed all over it; my fingernails and canine teeth jutted out sharp and deadly as I saw morbid fear on Raghav's face through my reddened eyes; the gathering ran helter-skelter as I growled upward at the thundering skies before wreaking havoc all over the Regal Lawns, hurling the bowl of Clafouti at the board of directors who now sat kneeling at my feet....

'And then, like I said,' he added, 'you did not even use professional colours in those bar graphs.'

I stood there open-mouthed with disbelief at Raghav's shameless admission of treachery.

14

The R Word

MEHEK THOUGHT I needed to calm down. The company needed me more than I needed it, she told me not for the first time. Of course I knew that. I was soon moving to a position where this plush consulting role would be but a secondary source of income for me that I could renounce at will. But what happened at the wedding was not a question of my desperation to latch on to the job. It was a dent to my prestige. And more importantly, it was a threat to the entire workforce. If they could do this to someone like me, the average employee who was less blessed with natural charisma, interfacing skills and general business acumen would be just a doormat for the organization. I was not fighting for myself. I was fighting for all of them.

For three days, nothing happened. I stayed at home expecting some sort of clarification. The only memo I got at the end of the third day was from the HR saying they would declare me an absconder if I stayed absent another day without providing an explanation or applying for leave as per the system.

Bastards.

I replied to them and gave a detailed account of what had transpired at the wedding. Five minutes later, Chirayu called and started apologizing again. But I was not willing to give these pathetic creatures another chance. Sorry, not happening, I said curtly and was about to hang up when he begged of me to at least come to the office once and meet him for the appraisal discussion. Sigh, that old trick of giving me a '1' rating and then hoping I'd let it go. If that was their trick they could go take a walk immediately, I said. But he insisted I wouldn't regret accepting his request, so I told him I'd come on the condition that he would keep it short, would spare me the hogwash, and would not touch his whiteboard marker at any cost. He giggled mysteriously and assured me everyone in the company respected my precious time and the discussion would be kept shorter than I could possibly anticipate.

The next morning when I reached work I found him standing outside the main door waiting for me. He folded his hands and bowed in greeting. He was either drunk at work, or trying to pull a fast one on me. By now it was getting a little clear that the latter was more likely. Then he told me he had ordered coffee from Starbucks for the discussion; did I want anything else? Cookies or cake? I got increasingly suspicious. This abnormality was disturbing. When he brought me to his cabin, I gawked on seeing Anand seated inside, waiting patiently for me.

Chirayu explained that given the situation of a prestigious, esteemed employee like me being a little upset with the company, as an exception both reviewer and appraiser were going to sit through this appraisal discussion together. But I was not to be so easily placated. After the wedding fiasco I planned to treat everything these people said with utter disregard and disbelief. I warned them that nothing would placate me this time, because I was seriously determined to question what should motivate me to continue working with this wretched company. Anand pacified me saying I would have enough time to vent my frustration, but only once they were done talking.

They spoke rapidly for the next ten minutes. They spoke a lot. I could see it in their eyes, I could hear it in their words. They were on the front foot already. I could already anticipate the next hook shot: *such dynamics occur in teamwork, why must a mature resource like you take this misunderstanding so serio...*

'And we regret to inform you that you have been accorded an appraisal rating of '3' for this financial year, but there is nothing that cannot be discussed,' Anand concluded.

I'm sorry? What? A '3'? Is this for real?

They read my mind and nodded. Chirayu added a grin to it. I kept reminding myself not to pick up that paperweight on his table and stone him to death. I held the paperweight silently and closed my fist. The blood in my veins was on simmer. The nerves on my temples were jutting out of my skin, ready to explode. Chirayu then continued in the same flattering tone that while I had always been a great performer and a smart thinker, it had lately come to their notice that I was not much of a team player. A case in point, they continued, was the recent wedding project where I may have deployed my ingenuity at work in early days and must have made the 'right kind of noises' in getting the contract with the caterers running, BUT!!

But a Byte was expected to go the larger distance and display Bytesphere's model code of consulting conduct by offering a helping hand to his other colleagues in the project, and more importantly, by seeing the project to its logical closure instead of running off on a foreign vacation.

At this point I began coughing violently as I tried screaming my lungs out to remind the duffers I had sought the approval of everyone and their aunt before going off on...and hold it, who would explain to the morons that the Swiss trip please not be called a junket; if anything, the company should have been acknowledging the fact that I had in a way represented them on an international podium of great repute and was soon on my way to being a published novelist of even greater repute.

Hearing this, Anand began to shed the friendly exterior that he had donned so far. *'Bokachoda!'* he bellowed, and angrily showed me a sub-clause of my contract with the company that stated I was not permitted to engage in any commercial venture without the prior consent of the organization, so if I were to harp one more time about my book contract, the consequences would not be pleasant. If anything, he countered, I needed to thank the company for keeping its mouth shut about my breach of contract.

'All said and done,' I stepped back a bit, 'my leave had received prior approval from everyone who mattered.'

Which was again not quite true, Chirayu explained with a pseudo-dejected expression. He reminded me of the pressure I had tried putting on the company, threatening them with a resignation letter and a related threat of pulling out from the potential contract with The Rembrandt. The company had little option but to let me go at that stage, he explained, because I was at a vantage point. Now that my vantage point was lost, Chirayu said, grinning ear to ear, they were now very keen to let me know once again who the real daddies were.

'And we might have condoned your irresponsible ways,' he continued, 'had you at least submitted your project report to us. But in a total lack of team spirit, you left everything to poor Raghav who, luckily, got every detail together and sent us this.'

They showed me the powerpoint presentation I had shared with Raghav on my pen drive. In his words, he had asked for it so that 'let's use it only for internal circulation until I fine tune it and make it crisper.' I skimmed through the slides in disgust. 'Let's make it crisper' could best be translated to 'let me change the fucking font of the title and make the pie charts 3D'. Usually known for my ready rebuttal and repartees, I was this time at a loss for words as it slowly sank in: Raghav was nothing but a crocodile in Armani. I knew I was fighting a lost battle now, but I weakly tried explaining that every word in the powerpoint presentation was mine. Except the 3D graphs and the sub-title that said 'Author: Raghav Krishnan.'

They smiled and said they would completely consider my argument if I could provide them with evidence supporting my claim; in the meantime as per company policies, they had taken a call to put me through a three-month fast-track reformatory programme that would help me overcome my professional hurdles via a daily tele-training programme called 'Goals Focus Rehabilitation', and making me more involved in teamwork via the 'Fostering Your *Esprit de Corps*' weekly workshop. After that they would monitor my improvement with the help of the 'Atomic Productivity Gradient' tool, and if my graph on the tool would display a continuously smooth trajectory towards the 'Inefficiency Burndown Zone', they would start looking for meaningful projects for me once again. In the meantime, Chirayu added, I could forget about the flexible work hours I had demanded, because as I could see, I was not deserving of such a luxury at this point and I needed to cooperate with the company in getting me back on my feet.

'Any questions?' their last question dripped irony.

I cleared my throat and took a large breath. They had wasted enough of my time and had totally ruined my mood. I'd keep it short. I started by telling them they could both go fuck themselves because the number of shits I gave to their appraisal rating was directly proportional to the amount of time I was further going to spend in that godforsaken office. And just in case they had thought barking dogs seldom bite, I was just about to *actually* bite them with my resignation; after that they were free to shove the Productivity Gradient tool up wherever they pleased.

Anand intervened, warning me I had better think through my decision. I laughed. Was he really so naïve? We were talking $50,000 here, boss. I hated being impolite, but this was the only language they were going to understand. So I told them about the book contract and about the potential signing amount which Bytesphere would never be able to afford to give me anyway. So they could do what they pleased to convince me otherwise, but this time my decision was firm.

'We accept,' Anand replied without waiting an extra

moment, and then turned to Chirayu. 'Accept his resignation in the system once he submits it. We must cooperate now that he knows what he is doing.' Chirayu giggled as they got up to leave. Anand turned back and told me he'd surely come see me at the launch of my book.

'By invite only,' I said, reclining in the chair and returning an ice-cold stare.

Once they were out of sight, I called the HR helpline to confirm if I would still be required to fulfil the three-month notice period before exiting, right? I mean, of course I still wanted to quit, but an extra three-month salary never hurt anyone. HR had no clue as usual. So I just got up and walked out of that hell-hole, but not before paying a flying visit to Raghav. The colour drained from his face when he saw me charge into his cabin. He stammered something, but I saved him the trouble by pinning him down to his seat and handing him a post-it note.

'My bank account details,' I said. 'You owe me. Would you like me to send you the amount, with interest, in a column graph format?' I did not need him to answer. It was satisfying enough to see the horrified look on his face. I slammed his door shut and walked out.

I was a free man now. I could not care less about the length of the notice period. Or maybe I did, just a little. I was also a little confused. I called Mehek and asked her if she could step out of her office and meet me for a quick lunch. I was not expecting her to, but she agreed—after checking her calendar. We met at Soam, off Marine Drive. Their dhoklas and sabudana khichdi were so delicious I could not speak for the first thirty minutes. Then I remembered what we had met for. I delivered the big news to her between mouthfuls of sabudana khichdi.

First she shrieked a little out of fright. Then she calmed down and started eating slowly. I asked her to say something. All she said was 'Hmm, ok.' That was not enough for me, so I asked her to say something more. Her eyes were talking a lot—alternating between 'I am proud of you I am sure you have thought this through' and 'What has this piece of shit done.' I was very confused, so I just quipped that her silence could probably be best assumed as cooperation. She nodded again in that mysterious way and then said, 'Just don't tell my parents.'

This request totally got my goat. Just when I thought I was letting my head clear up a bit, I flew into a rage again as we started arguing why her family had such lack of trust with regard to my decisions. In either case, I said, banging my fist on the table, I was proud of my decision and I would stand by it much as her parents would protest.

'You are overreacting, you need to calm down,' she said.

Oh no, I was damn right, I retorted. Her parents only needed an excuse to pull me down. Why couldn't I just call them and tell them I was now jobless so that they could grab the opportunity at once?

'You are overreacting, you need to calm down,' she repeated.

Oh no, I was not, I said again. People at a few nearby tables had quit eating and were looking at us with rapt expressions. I angrily told them to look to their food and then turned to Mehek again. Today I was going to speak. Today I was not going to be held back by what people thought of me. I had taken an independent decision for the first time in thirty years and I was going to cherish it. I was an artist and artists were moody, and moody talented artists should not be expected to subscribe to the tantrums of a mediocre organization they might unfortunately be trapped in.

'You are overreacting, you need to calm down NOW,' Mehek warned me and just then my phone rang. Brian had called to inform me that my manuscript, which he had played around with all these months, was now not palatable to any publisher and it needed some serious rework. For that, he suggested, I sign up for his customer delight package of $3000 wherein his team would help me remodel my characters, rework the plot line and hook points, and basically have his team write my book while I sat and watched the show. I told him that sounded like a fantastic idea and I would promptly call him back in Get-the-fuck-out-of-my-life hours.

There was stunned silence after I had hung up on him. Mehek looked at me open-mouthed in horror. I quietly reflected on what I had just done. Then I calmly paid the bill and escorted her out to her car.

'You had better know what you are doing,' she said as her driver turned on the engine before driving off.

Of course I knew what I was doing. For starters, I needed some fresh air and a fresh perspective. I drove my Sonata to Carter Road and parked myself in front of the ocean and laughed silently at the ironic ways of life. I must have been three when my parents taught me that any visiting guest who quizzed me about my ambitions must receive the response 'MBA!', if I wanted to escape eating broccoli and watching Rajesh Khanna's *Avatar* over the next three meals.

The word had become my answer before I had even figured

out what it meant, except what my parents had considered sufficient for me to know—that it made people rich. It sounded good enough to me, and I went ranting about my career aspirations in front of everyone; sometimes if a guest forgot to ask me the question, I would tap his knee and remind him.

Twenty years later when I earned my MBA degree, I still knew only that much about it—that it made you rich. In the twenty-fourth year of my life I actually realized this was not entirely true. However, it had laid out a life path for me that seemed just too good for me to even contemplate what other alternatives I could have chosen. And from there, ladies and gentlemen, emerged a maverick who rose above the banalities of an ordinary MBA; who dared to forgo the luxuries of an enviable salary and its associated plusses, the lure of those overseas assignments (which occasionally landed him in crisis but that could be overlooked considering the dollar multiplier); who finally embraced his true love for his art, irrespective of an evident lack of initial financial appeal. WHAT THE HELL HAD I JUST DONE I WANTED MY JOB BACK WOULD IT HELP IF I LAY PROSTATE AT CHIRAYU'S FEET AND OFFERED TO BECOME A DOORMAT SO HE COULD TRAMPLE OVER MY DIGNITY WITH ALL HIS CORPULENCE?

I hugged the leather interiors of my Hyundai Sonata and cried for some time. I would not say I had not thought this through already. With the kind of strategist I have proven myself to be in the past, I felt safe and smug about my decision and the path ahead. But sometimes when bullshit makes you feel warm and comfortable for too long, you get a little attached to the bullshit. It would take me a while to be willing to crawl out of the Bytesphere bullshit, feel the wind under my wings, and learn to fly again. I paused to take a few deep breaths. This was absurd. There was nothing to cry about.

I went home and lay in bed thinking of the next steps. I could not sleep. I finally picked up my phone and messaged Brian asking him if he had called me earlier in the day; my nephew was in the habit of manhandling my phone and had been up to some pranks lately, so...

I never heard from Brian again. Bah. Good riddance. I had a ready product and there were plenty of takers in the market. Patience would be the only key.

15

French Window, Mumbai Air

THE HR CALLED the very next day and asked me when I could come and surrender my identity card to them. I snapped at them saying I was busy and would call them back in an hour. Then I went to the toilet and during my morning ablutions I leisurely mulled over the repercussions of losing out on three months' salary. Emerging from the shower I concluded it would be a drop in the ocean. But by the time I called HR back I had also considered that an ocean comprised of many drops. So I curtly informed them that while my conscience did not even consider it imperative for me to call them back, I would have them know that because I was a stickler for discipline and professional commitment, I was willing to serve the company for the next three months before calling it quits.

'For old times' sake,' I said and then threw the ball in their court. They said that was very thoughtful of me, but the company had already decided to let me go. Very well. There was no time left to turn back and look at what once was. It was time to look forward. And one key aspect of looking forward without looking at the past with any regrets was to cut down on my expenses. I knew this was not going to be easy because I had got used to a high disposable income at an age when I had been very raw. But I would have to change with the times.

And I did not even have to try all that hard. When I returned from Bytesphere for the last time, I saw a truck parked outside my apartment. A man called Gopi flashed a real estate broker's card and introduced his team of luggage handlers, saying he had instructions from Mehek. I called her and she said it was the least she could do, but her tone made clear she was still to come to terms with my predicament. She wanted me to move in with her into her sea-facing apartment at Bandstand!

For a minute I totally forgot about my unfounded fears and did a mental cartwheel at the thought of vacating my matchbox apartment at Dadar's Chamunda Cooperative Housing Society and moving into Mehek's approximately eighty-bedroom modular apartment—a move that possibly indicated my decision was reaping rich dividends already! Of course all I told her was how embarrassed I was at the very thought of leaning on her for support, but luckily she wanted to hear none of that and forced me to pack up that very instant. So I got Gopi's men to help me vacate the Chamunda apartment and to load the luggage into their truck, after which they asked me for Rs 2100. I negotiated a bargain citing potential repeat services, but Gopi insisted it was a standard company quote that he could not tinker with, but he told me he could help me with future brokering services at cheaper prices if I contacted him directly. I immediately saved his number on speed dial.

Later at Mehek's apartment, I once again made suitable noises against her insistence I move in with her. I spoke of pride, honour and some other such stuff that I did not really believe in to be honest. She comforted me and said she had insisted only because she thought this move would benefit me, but she totally understood if my pride was being hurt and that she would not protest if I wanted to move back to Chamunda and deal with this change on my own terms.

I immediately got up from the couch, grabbed her by the shoulders and assured her I would honour her sentiments by continuing to stay with her. But there would be some conditions. I would not sit smugly in a plush house paid for by her company, without bothering to contribute towards the household in any way. And by a little bit of God's grace and mostly because of my prudence and stately bank statements, I had a lot of money saved up that would come to good use. She told me not to worry, that she had it all figured out. I would pick up all costs pertaining to household utilities and groceries, while she would bear the monthly wages of the maid and her driver and also of any entertainment avenues we explored outside over weekends.

With my sense of self-guilt now out of the way, I worried myself a bit about what my parents would think of my decision. Because I could not have withheld the information forever, I decided to tell them about it in the most logical, rational and mature manner possible.

'We would love to hear your point of view,' they said, upon hearing the news. This was usually their opening gambit and a prelude to a major calamity befalling me. I remember carrying my mathematics answer sheet home after my class ten prelims to show my parents that I had scored a seventy-nine on hundred. They told me they wanted to first hear my point of view. I told them my point of view was that I could have scored a lot more were it not for some silly mistakes I had made while answering the test. To which my father muttered, 'And our point of view is that you were born because of a silly mistake!' So this time, I trod the path of caution and leaked the details slowly, making sure not to let my guard down.

Having tolerated me for thirty years they had now mellowed greatly, which they attributed to my being an adult; but was actually because I had carved out a fine career (so far). Naturally, the news of the resignation did not go down well. I received a short lecture, which went over three identical cycles that began with the sentence 'It is our fault only,' made an interlude at 'When we were your age we understood responsibility', and ended with 'Anyway you are very smart do what you want.' I thought it best to let all supplementary information, such as my having moved in with Mehek, be. None of us could have handled any more honesty for the day.

Over the next three months, I was driven to the brink of insanity by a variety of reasons. For starters, I was rejected by nine publishers. Surprisingly all nine wrote to me saying how much they enjoyed reading the synopsis, but it just did not meet their requirements. Those emails were like slow bombardments from the camp of diplomacy. Some others were more frank, and sent automated replies saying they were booked out for as long as I could imagine and that maybe I could try my luck again in 2017.

These early rejections would not have upset me were it not for the collective urge of the entire world to not mind its own business and to keep asking me 'So how does it feel like to have quit your job?' I know those questions were always asked with a sense of awe—I was probably the first person in my MBA batch to have had this novel idea of quitting my job and everyone was very impressed. But their questions always made me feel like it was some sort of disease I had contracted. Some of those shameless fellows had pictures of themselves with their Lamborghinis, with the London Eye and what not in the background and kept prodding me to promise them that I would send them free copies of the book once it was out. Tired, I finally had to stop using the social network altogether.

Skype conversations with my to-be father-in-law did not stop though, and each conversation was a minefield. I could never Skype him from the apartment, because all hell would break loose if he knew, said Mehek. What about that overnighter in Goa then, on the fight-as-you-drive trip to Mysore? Did her father really think we had a platonic relationship then? Anyway, I was also faced with the delicate responsibility of not letting him know I was now jobless; I had to hold him off at least till my first novel was published and I had received my first fat royalty cheque.

So every time he demanded that we chat, I would drive down to my old favourite café and chat with him for hours. And because the café no longer allowed patrons to occupy tables without shelling out big bucks, I would have to order a black coffee each time I went in. One black coffee—a cup of hot water and some coffee beans—for Rs 116. I was beginning to fail to understand the ways of this world, seriously.

Mehek was the only balancing factor that helped me reclaim myself during these testing times—except the times she kept the living room's split air conditioner on for no discernible reason. We had split the costs and she was being very nice by treating me to movies (the *Himmatwala* and *Heropanti* types) occasionally; but I was unable to understand what six air conditioners, one dishwasher, one washing machine and one dryer were doing in an apartment occupied by only two people.

One day I quit hesitating (I hesitated out of cowardice and courtesy), and asked her outright what she thought of opening the gigantic French windows that overlooked the Arabian Sea so we could soak in some fresh, free-of-cost air. She rolled her eyes in horror and told me those French windows would always remain closed, because salty sediment from the sea blew in and deposited itself on her head and turned her hair dull and lifeless.

On that sensitive note, I put myself to sleep for another night of anxiety-filled dreams.

Santro

I WAS SO excited I could not believe I was seeing this day in my lifetime! I jumped out of bed on receiving the news and darted out of the building on to the sea face, screaming my lungs out in ecstasy. When I could run no longer, I sat down and caught my breath, and then put up the news on the social network so that people could stop asking me the same question over and over again.

The last seven months had felt like a lifetime of commuting on a Virar fast train. I had been taken for a ride now and again. I had withstood sweat and grime in trying to visit publishing houses—first to negotiate, then to plead—and had lived with that constant feeling that Virar would never arrive and that I would be on the train forever. Virar had arrived.

Swarup from something known as Sunrise Publishers had called me that morning asking if I would be willing to publish my first book with them. Of course my first question to him was how had Sunrise figured out I needed a publisher, because I could not for the life of me remember having contacted them.

He explained that his firm worked on its mission statement of making the best of waste (not sure what he meant by that), which is why they sourced manuscripts that had been panned and rejected by editorial boards of other companies. Their contacts in other publishing houses helped them procure such waste material. After patiently listening to him for ten minutes and thanking him for his offer, I politely asked him to stop calling my work 'waste material'. He laughed and quipped it was nothing to feel bad about for even the smelliest mud pond could help a lotus bloom or something. I realized it would be in the interest of my mental health to keep this conversation as short as possible and to discuss our terms of agreement.

'What terms of agreement?' he wanted to know.

I told him about my abandoned contract of $50,000 with Crown, in response to which he started laughing like a maniac. After regaining sobriety he told me he would offer me a 7 per cent royalty on every copy sold—besides taxes as usual. This time I laughed in equal measure but only until I realized he was serious. So I told him I would consider his proposal with due sincerity and would get back to him with a response soon. After that I spoke to Mehek who was in alignment with my hunch that it would be a very bad decision to try and throw my weight around given the drought of options. Ten minutes later I called Swarup and told him I accepted his offer because as an artist I valued the admiration of my work more than the moolah it would fetch me (and also because some money was better than the zero money I had made in the last 7 months, though I did not mention this). I was fine with the 7 per cent royalty as long as the signing amount made up for this disappointing figure. To which he replied that he did not give out signing amounts to any writer, *leave alone to me*, God knows why he needed to add that last bit—I was fed up of this man even before having met him.

Alright, no signing bonus then. I would just have to make do with an advance component of a lakh or two against my future royalties I said, in response to which he started chanting 'no' even before I could complete my sentence. My royalties would be dispatched to me once a year, depending on how many copies had sold.

'Just send me the contract and I will sign it,' I sighed finally.

Desperate measures called for signing unacceptable terms. As it was I had taken a lot of unacceptable events over the last seven months in my stride. For instance, the first quarterly electricity bill of the apartment Mehek handed to me to deal with, which alone had the potential to wreck my mind. My most painful moment of that phase was when Mehek first broached the suggestion that I do away with my prized Hyundai Sonata. I had first vehemently opposed the idea. We fought over it. I told her it was a symbol of my status and I would not part with it. She said I no longer had the status I was talking about and that I needed to be more practical. I cried a little over this insensitive remark. Of course then she apologized and said she did not mean it but I was very inconsolable, and so she offered to go get the groceries herself that month, after which I felt somewhat better. But over time I began seeing sense in the idea of doing away with the car. For one, the goddamn expenses never seemed to cease. Secondly, the Sonata no longer looked like a Sonata. It looked like an aged, sad rock that had caved in under an avalanche of bird poop.

The first time I noticed this ugly sight was when I was seated at a window contemplating the state of affairs in my life, and I noticed my car parked outside the society gates in a condition that completely aligned with my then state of affairs. The stupid birds had to use only my Sonata as a commode? Couldn't they show some class?

Fine, I would sell it. But Mehek had already done so much for me by allowing me into her apartment and by supporting me during this challenging phase of my life. Would it not be unfair if I now used her company-provided, chauffeur-driven Skoda to ferry me to and from the café for my daily writing sessions and chats with her father, not to mention those visits to publishing houses? She clarified she only meant that I sell off the Sonata and start travelling by bus instead.

That would not happen. I would not trade a Sonata for a BEST bus. So six months ago I finally decided to trade it for a less classy car. If the birds needed a commode, they could have another one—not my Sonata. Gopi assured me he could get my Sonata exchanged for a second-hand Hyundai Santro. This sounded acceptable to me. He said he had a buyer in mind to whom I could sell my Sonata for a sum of eight lakh. A second-hand Santro could be sold to me in under a lakh. The profit margin was too enticing to let go. So one morning I woke up and asked the car cleaner if he could make my Sonata look a little presentable. He looked at it pitiably and said it would cost me six hundred bucks. I explained I only needed him to wash it right there with a hose pipe, he didn't need to take it for a dip in the Arabian Sea. He stood his ground. I thanked him and asked him to leave, then pulled out a hose pipe and tearfully gave a farewell shower to my car.

Three hours later, I had handed it over to Gopi in return for a Santro that he guided me to in his showroom. The car was around one-tenth the size of my previous car and looked like it had traversed every nook, corner and pothole of Andheri East and Kurla. There were around four dents, twelve scratches and one cracked glass pane on its tubby little body. This car had seen struggle. It would fit with my image given my current disposition. I told Gopi I did not care about trivial issues, I was happy with what I saw. I just wanted to sign the papers, be done with all the formalities and then drive away.

He gleefully took me inside his office, got me to sign the papers for both the deals, and handed me a cheque for seven lakh. His staff, grinning ear to ear, looked mighty pleased too. Gopi then handed me the keys to my new (I mean, new in my possession) car and escorted me outside. I tried opening the door to get inside the car, but it wouldn't relent. I pulled at it with both my hands till it yielded a short, painful creak but yet refused to open.

'Careful!' Gopi ordered, escorting me to the co-passenger's side of the car. He then regrettably explained there were some intermittent mechanical issues with the door on the driver's side which had rendered its behaviour unpredictable —so it would be best if I got in through the co-passenger's side and crawled my way over to the driver's seat. I looked at Gopi incredulously, but he shrugged and said this was the cheapest deal he could get me. Well, a minor obstacle again, I told myself. With the kind of obscurity I had been living in of late, I was not too worried about people watching me crawl like a reptile inside a car before driving it. I then navigated my body—which had been variously referred to by friends as 'fat', by subordinates as 'you are only healthy boss' and by Mehek's father as 'do you eat only butter as your main meal'—through the minimal breadth of the car. It took me around fifteen minutes to settle into my seat, after which Gopi pulled out a paperweight from the glove compartment and handed it to me. I asked him what it was for. He tapped the hand brake and said it sometimes felt tempted to bring itself down after being applied. While he had been unable to find an immediate solution, he reckoned that placing the paperweight under the groin of the hand brake would ensure there would be no untoward release of the brake when the car was parked.

Well, anything goes as long as the car moves, I reckoned. Now that I was finally getting published, I was tempted to do away with the Santro. I had used it for six months and I was very clear I had had enough. Every time I drove it I felt its chassis going further down towards the ground. The poor thing was not able to take my weight any more. But I had burnt my fingers by trusting that joker Brian once, and so I was measuring my success with Sunrise Publishers with a note of caution. As it is I had never heard of Sunrise Publishers earlier, so there was no clear reason to be ecstatic about signing a contract with them anyway. I looked them up on Google. Only thirteen results came up. Man, I had more Google results than that come up in my name without my having accomplished anything significant. Fine, at least their website had some meaningful information I could ruminate on: they had published three books so far, all non-fiction. The first was a travelogue written by a Romanian tourist's travails in India. The second was a collection of poems only English teachers could read and comprehend. The third was—I did not stop to read the blurb—titled *The Four Mistakes of My Life*. I did not get a nice vibe from any of these books. Sure enough, when I looked them up I got no significant results on Google either. Swarup laughed when I called him to share my apprehension. He said this was because they served a very niche segment of the reading market in India, but their books had been doing very well within that niche segment. I nervously asked him what that niche segment was.

'Government and corporate libraries,' he said. 'And lately, the collection of poems has also made it to school curricula.'

I congratulated him for that significant progress but added that my book did not serve any of these audiences and I needed to connect with the masses. My story had a broader outreach and I needed private retailers to stock it by the thousands.

'Of course,' he said, 'that is where you will pitch in.'

'What does that mean?' I asked, unsure of what he wanted from me.

He suggested I needed to start building a relationship with these private retailers: talking to them about my book and convincing them to start stocking it once it was ready. I also needed to build myself as a brand; brand creation leads to brand awareness leads to brand demand leads to brand success leads to brand value. I told him I was very comfortable with his first suggestion of building a relationship with retailers; after all smooth talking people into getting my job done was all that had always differentiated me from all other Bytes who only played business by the book. But I was not very sure what he meant by the brand building exercise, especially when my book was not yet out.

'Make people look forward to your book coming out soon,' he said. 'When the book is finally ready to release, those people should be flocking to the stores ransacking them looking for a copy.'

I felt a rush of blood course through my veins. Yes!! This was what needed to happen. I had to capture the mind space of the reading millions. I needed them to go berserk in anticipation of the book. I needed to seduce them with all the waiting. And once the book was out, there would be pandemonium, not a mere phenomenon in the making. Nakul Kapoor had to be made synonymous with literature. Women needed to pass out with delirium on seeing me at my book launch. I was happy now, and charged up.

'Three lakhs for a month,' Mehek told me about a public relations firm she had enquired about, after I had briefed her about my conversation with Swarup. Bloody hell, what was I to do next? Sell off that Santro and buy a Tobu cycle in exchange? My enormous savings from the job at Bytesphere were depleting fast, and I needed to be wiser than spending them on some PR exercise over a period of a month. On second thoughts, I did not need the brand building exercise. My work would speak for itself.

17

You Deserve a Discount

'WHY DON'T YOU give meditation a try?' Mehek asked me for the ninety-ninth time that month when she saw me pick up a fallen cookie and wash it under the tap because I had probably confused it with an apple. She thought I needed help. I thought she needed to stop saying that so often. But yes, I needed help.

It had taken Sunrise Publishers six months to publish my novel, during which time I had nearly forgotten what a sunrise felt like. There was gloom and doom all around. It had been over a year since I had quit my job and the only thing that I had been proud of in these thirteen months was the sheer skill with which I had hidden the truth about my joblessness from my spy of a father-in-law to-be. He would Skype me almost every alternate day and would often ask me why I always Skyped from a café, 'and when do you go to work?' he asked me after barely holding in his pent-up curiosity for some weeks.

I told him something about a flexible work schedule that the company had allowed only special employees like me and that I liked working in open, cubicle-free environments such as cafés because they enhanced my productivity. He said he was keen to see what my office cubicle looked like and that I should Skype him the following day from my cubicle. I told him Skype was blocked in my office. He told me he would ask the local police inspector to speak to my office IT team to have it unblocked for me. He nearly had me there, but I quickly told him I was going to be away on an official conference plus follow-up visits and would Skype with him on returning. That held him off until the next time, but his suspicion was now peaking.

Meanwhile, the book was ready, and yet not quite so—something like that constipated situation where something almost comes out and then stays put because, well, well tried but you needed to try harder. Thanks to the wonderful lack of strategy on part of Sunrise, I now knew why their three books had not sold enough to make it to Google search results. And I now knew what Swarup had meant when he said they catered to a 'niche' market.

What was my book about?

It was a corporate executive's narrative of inspiring and sometimes sordid stories at his workplace.

Who would want to read such a story?

The working class, the salaried, cost-conscious employees of India.

What had Sunrise priced the book at?

All of Rs 495.

Boss. That was equivalent to buying ten kilos of onions. Why would anyone buy a book for that price? I expressed my doubts to Swarup who rudely brushed them off saying he understood the business better than I did.

Now a month since the book had been published, it had not made it to a single store. 'But we have sent it to some online portals and all government libraries and we are getting a good response,' Swarup assured me, after which my brain wanted to implode.

Because Swarup firmly believed that he had met his target audience and his job was pretty much done there, I had to personally start making courtesy calls to various bookstores and pleading with them to give the book a chance. In these thirteen months my ego had died a thousand deaths, so I was not very taken aback when my calls were not addressed by anyone.

I finally relented to hiring a public relations agent. And going by the kind of amounts some agents had quoted earlier, I was most certain I could afford them only if Papa Gupta asked some police inspector to speak to them and drill some considerate sense into them. And then I remembered, Raghav still owed me money! I called that bastard thrice a day for three days and not a single phone call was answered. He had disappeared from the face of the earth.

'Let me pump in some money,' Mehek said. 'It might be worth the effort after all.'

I was now even tired of pretending that I did not want to lean on her for financial support. So I asked her to transfer whatever money she could to my bank account and she could have my goodwill in return. After a week of pottering around, I received a call from a public relations firm that claimed it would have all the private retailers on their knees begging for the book.' That is the kind of wave we will create in the media,' they promised me.

I paid a visit to their office the same afternoon. I had some trouble getting past the main gate because the security guard saw my Santro and wanted to send me to the rear of the building where deliveries were made to the godown. He almost threw up when I told him I was a potential client. He looked me up and down before finally directing me to a parking area flooded with the kind of cars I had always dreamed of owning when I had been selected for my MBA course and had owned one only to sell it off in exchange for this battered little Santro that convinced the guard I had come to deliver bulk stationery.

The only vacant bay between two flashy sedans had just enough space for an auto rickshaw to deposit itself. 'That much should be enough for you,' he said before returning to the gate.

It took me twenty minutes to crawl out of the driver's seat and get out of the other side of the car. In the process the door of the Santro rammed into the BMW parked next to it. This resulted in the shape of the Santro changing even further, which had ceased to matter to me. But what really troubled me was that I was a pool of sweat by now. I cooled down for a few minutes in the lobby before taking the lift up to the PR office.

A team of very enthusiastic PR agents accosted me right at the gate and escorted me straight into a meeting room where they ran me through a presentation of 345 slides, plus an appendix. And it looked like they were fresh out of college, because they began every slide with 'As is self-explanatory on this slide.'

I was not leading a particularly busy life these days, so I

tried paying attention for as long as I could, before my eyes began shutting involuntarily. One of the agents then asked me if I would like to have something. Actually, I had been hoping they would ask me, because our maid had not shown up that morning and Mehek had told me I would need to get lunch outside. So I said that if they insisted I wouldn't mind a chicken club sandwich, a bag of fries and some coffee. They looked at each other and convened outside, probably wondering where to arrange a chicken club sandwich from, embarrassing me no end in that time. Then two of them came inside to resume the presentation and laughed it off saying, 'No worries, it will all be here soon.'

Over the next six hours or so, they told me everything they could do for me: ranging from media coverage to television panel discussions to online content management. And the price was quoted on the last slide: seven lakh for a year. I burped a little on the club sandwich and told them all I needed was some basic buzz to be created until the book made it to the stores and then the book could anyway work its charm. They had the audacity to laugh at my suggestion before arguing that their actual support would be needed only *after* the book had made its way into the stores. Oh.

So I would still have to get it into the stores then. Before my head could begin pounding, they said they would begin with an official book-launch event at one of the bookstores. That would automatically ensure the store would hoard copies. In all likelihood, the other stores would follow suit. All they needed from my side was a chief guest who could attract some media attention while saying good things about my book, and then they would take care of the rest. Because I had few other options, I agreed to their proposal and signed the contract for a year. The jubilant agents then escorted me down to the car park. This made me very awkward because I was very possessive about my Santro and was not keen to let them take a look at it. But they wouldn't hear a word. Once in the car park, I shook hands with all of them and said I would take it from here and they could carry on with their work. My car was right in front of us and I could walk up to it alone, I said pointing in the general direction of a few big cars which *actually* looked like cars. They stuck to me like glue as I awkwardly made the long walk towards the bird scat-laden Santro. There it was, sandwiched humbly between a BMW and a Skoda. If getting out of the car in that crammed space had been a challenge, it now seemed impossible to get back in.

After staring at the machine in absolute wonder, one of the agents went behind it and gave it a gentle push with a couple of his fingers. The car painfully creaked forward like a baby that cries on being woken up. About a dozen employees of various offices, who were at a nearby tea stall, turned towards the source of the sound. The agent prodded the car with his fingers a little more till it finally came out of the parking bay and stood in front of us, swaying a little in the gentle wind. I shook hands with them once again, hoping they would leave me alone now. But they stood there smiling. So I reluctantly opened the door from the passenger's side and saw the amazement on their faces from the corner of my eye as I moved like a giant snake over to the driver's seat. I rolled down the window and observed them look at each other with expressions of extreme pity.

'Sir, we are willing to give you a discount,' one of them said finally. 'We will send you a revised contract for five lakh for the year.'

I thanked them and drove off into the traffic, mentally apologizing to them for the kilogram of black smoke my Santro farted into their faces as I left. And I also silently thanked the Santro. For all the embarrassment it had caused me, it had at least saved me two lakh.

18

Inner Peace

'YOU WERE MUMBLING in your sleep again last night,' Mehek told me the day I received a courier from Sunrise Publishers. With trembling fingers I ripped it open. There it lay in front of my eyes: the single biggest thing I had made a brouhaha out of, which had cost me my job and was most certainly going to cost me a lot of money going forward—if there was something that compensated for all the agony, it was the excitement of seeing it finally in its complete form.

The Chaos Project – by Nakul Kapoor, said the text in bold against a magenta background. Enclosed was a note from Swarup asking me for feedback on the look and feel of the book. I was too overwhelmed to respond, not only because of the sight of the book but also because Mehek had already repeated for the third time that I had been talking a lot in my sleep lately. Given the frequency with which she had been reporting these anomalies in my sleep patterns, I was quite convinced she was making up these stories so I could be talked into joining that meditation programme and she could hence utilize that free voucher from the meditation camp her colleague Aniket had gifted her. Little did she know that this Aniket fellow was a major reason why I probably was in need of these meditation classes in the first place.

Aniket Shah was some sort of poet who had lost his way to salvation and had landed up at Goldman Sachs in the process. He had fallen head over heels in love with Mehek at work although he would never admit it. This was evident even to me who had never had the misfortune of meeting him, by the desperation with which he used to call her every night after dinner and tell her how purposeless life was without a caring partner and some such shit. No, I was not threatened by this chap the way I had once been by that six-pack macho doll Sameer Kashyap. But I had a problem with the way Aniket transferred his melancholy to Mehek's apartment with his phone call every night, thus in the process driving me crazy and worried about my own future. His latest addition to my problems was this meditation voucher he had handed to Mehek as some sort of goodwill gesture. And because it was a voucher for two and Mehek did not want to go with Aniket (thank God for small mercies), she was now coaxing me into coming along.

'Fine, I will come along,' I finally relented in order to get the monkey off my back more than any other purpose I could possibly imagine meditation would serve to my peace of mind.

My indifference to the meditation camp lasted only until we entered the meditation hall. It felt like the first day at college when I had spotted Sneha Mehta's fallen handkerchief and I had run behind her to return it, and sensed our head of department running after me because it was his handkerchief that had fallen, but this part is not important. Sagarika was our meditation instructor. She was slender, graceful, warm, and every bit the voyeuristic desire of every single man and of other men who were otherwise committed to their partners but occasionally drifted pushed by temporary eddies of distraction owing to the turbulence in their lives and their desire to have a yoga-sculpted delicate shoulder to cry on. I immediately took Mehek to a corner of the room, held her by the arms and thanked her for bringing me here because I was feeling better already. Then I told her that in order for me to properly reap the benefits of the camp, it was imperative that I concentrate solely on the process of meditation rather than fooling around with her. And so it was necessary that we both sat as far from each other as possible through the entire duration of this camp, and I sprinted to the front row and deposited myself right in front of Sagarika.

Eventually I surmised that the woman was some sort of magician. Even after a hectic yoga-aerobics session, her leotards drenched in sweat, she smelled enviably fragrant. Divine powers. Her smile was actually enough for me to attain rejuvenation and possibly also salvation, but I chose to comply with the entire exercising routine she put us through. Her approach of doing a one-on-one with each student so she could feel their pulse and heal them with the touch of her velvet fingers and (possibly) her lily-scented perfume was very refreshing and endearing. I could not open up to her over the first couple of classes, because I could feel Mehek's gimlet eyes on me from her corner of the room during my one-on-one. The third day onwards, I told Mehek I would be attending the sessions in the afternoon going forward.

'Why?' she asked suspiciously.

Arre boss because I need to open up before Sagarika (mentally) which I cannot do with you hovering over me, is what I wanted to say. But I simply said, 'Because the afternoon between 3.00 and 4.00 p.m. is when I am least productive and I want Sagarika to tackle my mental block at precisely that time. And I don't want you to leave work midway and join me.'

Sagarika was brilliant. She sat on the floor with her legs crossed, took my hands in hers, asked me to close my eyes and to relay all my troubles to her. I allowed this moment to last forever. I mean I had too many troubles to talk about to be able to keep the conversation short. 'Not a problem,' said Sagarika, and I could hear her comforting smile.

'I am all ears.' But where was I to begin? I was frustrated, anxious and angry all at once. I was frustrated primarily on account of my own overestimation of what a novelist's life was likely to be. The repeated mention of the $50,000 that finally never reached me had rendered me ecstatic, arrogant, and finally jobless. And while I was otherwise a very mature, sensitive man who was not sexist by any measure, I had been secretly growing insecure by Mehek's meteoric rise at Goldman Sachs.

I had no idea what that woman ate at lunch but she seemed to be a powerhouse of energy always willing to shed that extra bit of intellect oozing off her on to Goldman Sachs. The company had crowned her Best Employee of the Year and I had tried very hard to look excited about it but had howled and cried my heart out, and mentally I had sold her gold medal at the black market so I could pay off the electricity and utility bills for the month.

I was also increasingly anxious about the future of our

relationship, because going by the suspicion and inquisitorial tones in her father's voice it would not be too long before he figured out I had been feeding off his daughter's earnings for over a year. He had considered me little better than an insect when I had been an exemplary role model for every Indian corporate executive, and I shuddered at the thought of what he would think of me now.

I was also anxious because I was now suddenly not as confident about my skills as a novelist, given the way it was tottering around government libraries and obscure online retailers without making its way into the bookstores that really mattered. Also, the royalty quotes that Sunrise had offered me were enough reason for me to decide to take up one of those Bytespherish hackneyed jobs again. That would totally be the death of my self-respect after having told every living soul in existence that I was above the trivialities of a corporate job and that I had better avenues to look up to. But if I were to choose between my self-respect and my ability to buy myself my bread, I was probably going to tilt towards the latter.

'And what are you angry about?' Sagarika softly asked.

I inhaled the fragrance of her breath and momentarily forgot what I was angry about. I breathed deeply and smiled before I realized I still needed to look suitably upset so we could continue talking. I told her I was angry with almost everyone around me, but would like to particularly mention that ass Brian for having guzzled up thousands of my dollars for nothing and also for making me see a dream that was supposed to be reserved only for someone like JK Rowling. But if there was only one person that I had to keep on my hit list, it would be that uber fucker Raghav, whom I had once made the mistake of nearly idolizing. The man had turned out to be a scheming rat with privileged membership at The Hyatt who had absconded with a gargantuan amount of money I had lent him in good faith and out of humanity.

'Can you do something about it?' she asked, gently placing her delicate, small hands on my calloused skin. I cringed, feeling my own rough skin rub against her petal-soft hands, but then I suddenly felt very nice about that touch in a mostly non-sexual way. I clasped her palms tighter and tried very hard to cry so that we could repeat this routine a few more times.

Meanwhile, to answer her question, of course there was something I could do about it. I could sneak into his house in the dead of the night, stuff all his credit cards into his mouth and then choke him to death. She ran her fingers along mine and said she was sure I was not the murderous kind, because I had a pure heart....

How did she know? We were clearly forming a connection. She also assured me my book would be a stupendous success but for that to happen I needed to stop worrying myself sick and to start focusing on the job at hand, which was promoting the book in whatever way I could. Then she asked if she could help me with anything else. I just wanted to submit my helplessness to the magic that lay in her hands. I just wanted catharsis so I could vent out my angst and go home a happier person. But I was conscious of the fact that she had others waiting for their one-on-one sessions and my catharsis would take time. So while I was otherwise not of the disposition to indulge in any sort of entertainment, I was game to join her for dinner someplace quiet where she could guide me to the road on which light did shine. Our conversation ended abruptly soon after. But I thanked her for her time and suggested we could reconvene next time and chalk out a plan.

Things began looking up the very next day. I guess I needed to meet Sagarika more often after all. The PR agents called with the wonderful news that a bookstore with the reputation of being one of the oldest in Mumbai (and now on the verge of shutting down, although this information was withheld from me) had agreed to launch my book amidst a grand media event—as long as I arranged for a celebrity chief guest who could attract the media to the store. At least one bookstore in the country would now have my book showcased; not a bad start, I thought. So I jubilantly put up notices all over the social media, carefully ducking the same ridiculous questions about free copies. One of those funny guys asking for a free copy was actually holidaying with his wife in the Bahamas, shameless fellow. I felt like blocking him permanently.

My parents were very delighted to hear about the book launch. They had not spoken to me for the last few months partly because they had no more hope from me and partly because they were aware I was on the verge of a nervous breakdown and it was not humanly possible for them to utter anything that would make me feel less miserable about the future of my career. I was a little unhappy when they told me they wouldn't be able to attend the event because of my father's official tour somewhere in Bali. I must point out I wasn't unhappy because they wouldn't be there, but because even my parents were travelling to exotic destinations at a time when I was struggling every day to make ends meet. Daddy Gupta also called to say that they would not be able to make it to the event. This was certainly no reason for me to feel upset. In fact I felt almost grateful. Imagine Daddy Gupta arriving at the event in a police staff car, all sirens blazing—it would not have boded well for the mood of the event.

The only people I *really* wanted at this event were the senior management at Bytesphere. This was after all the moment, the anticipation of which had inspired me to finally free myself from their wretched claws. I sent them a stinker of an email invite. Chirayu congratulated me in response and said he always knew I had the potential to make the scene. And then, believe it or not, he asked me if he could get a free copy too. The bastard had the kind of money that could have printed the book for me and marketed it too, and he wanted a free copy. I did not care to respond.

The next day I paid a visit to the bookstore to finalize the modalities of the event. And the sight of what lay at the entrance completely blew the wind out of me. Copies of a book were stacked like a giant pyramid at the entrance. 'Runaway bestseller,' a placard next to the pyramid declared. Customers streamed in, picking up a copy each and proceeding to the cash counter. I followed suit and inched closer to the pyramid. The title of the book, what may have been on the cover—everything was a blur. My eyes were transfixed on the picture and the name of the man who had written what was apparently selling like hot cakes: Shivang Apte.

This was fantastic news; very heartening to find the face of a genial, kind, well-meaning and ambitious acquaintance on the covers of his dream project. Everyone on the face of this earth was becoming a highly acclaimed author and here I was, struggling to give my novel the space it deserved. I hated Shivang Apte. Maybe now I could ask him to reimburse me for that ride in the limousine and for the dinner at *Tastes of India*. Or at least he could offer to meet me and spill the beans on how his book was making me feel like the unwanted stepchild of the Indian fiction market.

I looked up his contact and sent him an email saying it had been quite a while since we'd caught up, and that it was great to know he had finally found his true calling, and, I casually added, I was about to release my first novel too—just so he knew he was talking to a peer.

I hovered around the store a while after I was done talking to the manager, just to see what was so fabulous about Shivang Apte. Maybe just pure luck. I couldn't tell what made him click. But I do know that I was annoyed beyond belief when two girls barged into the store and squealed with delight seeing the copies of his book before picking up one each and kissing it.

I ambled over to them and casually quipped that Apte was known to me because he had sought writing advice from me at a writer's symposium; wasn't it ironical that his book released before mine, although that could be because I had refused to settle for just another run-of-the-mill publisher. The girls looked at each other and then at me with an absolute lack of interest and respect, before getting Apte's mediocre work billed at the counter and leaving the store.

I must admit Mehek was amazingly supportive during the anxious days leading to the event. She took us out to dinner more often and she talked less and less about Goldman Sachs.

In fact, she had even stopped taking Aniket's calls, at least in my presence. I felt a little guilty about my increased meditation sessions with Sagarika but then in a way I was doing this for Mehek—my spiritual and mental well-being was a step forward in the prosperity of our relationship. And it wasn't as though I was having a scene with Sagarika or something, unless by chance such an opportunity arose, in which case I would have to take some very tough decisions. But those decisions were still likely to tilt in favour of Mehek because she had been at her best behaviour ever since I had moved into her apartment—except for the times she harped on how much she wanted the old me back. The first few times I found it very endearing because I thought she was referring to the radiant youthfulness and boyish charm I once used to exude that she wanted back. I thought that was very considerate and compassionate. Then she finally told me that what she meant was that I probably needed to consider taking up a job again.

It started with a healthy debate on the dining table eating pasta made with unnecessarily organic oil which I was made to buy for seven hundred rupees at every grocery trip. I explained that going back to a job with my qualifications and credentials was never going to be a big deal. But it would be a humiliating defeat for the very conviction I had about myself a year ago. She asked me to choose between my conviction and my future.

Oh, I see. I got up, partly because I was upset with what she was insinuating with the suggestion and partly because that pasta tasted like the remnants of a bowl of Cerelac. I could totally see what she was getting at—that she did not think I was going to make a fine career out of writing. I mean, even I had begun to harbour some fears, but how dare she say it aloud? Was I turning out to be a big financial burden on her, some sort of liability? Or was I just not good enough to be boyfriend to a Goldman Sachs dream-chaser? She said I was overreacting and all that she meant was I look for a job in the writing space itself so it could supplement my creativity alongside helping me pay my bills. Oh, right! So the bills were all it was about.

'Guess what will help me pay my bills?' I asked, getting up. 'That we don't live in an apartment with six airconditioners, one washer, one dryer, one dishwasher, and I don't know, what—five televisions?' I said with my decibel level rising with each word. 'Even the Ambanis must be using lesser electricity at Antilla! I SOMETIMES FEEL LIKE I LIVE IN A CROMA SHOWROOM!'

I saw her quiver with rage. This either meant that she was going to cry or that she was going to kill me, none of which I was prepared for. So I angrily stormed into the bedroom, opened my suitcase as noisily as possible, in the hope that she would come running into my arms and apologize for trying to make me realize what was actually in my best interests. I collected my clothes with one clean sweep of the wardrobe shelf, threw them in and shut the suitcase lid. Then I walked out into the living room, making sure each step could be loudly heard to mark my vehement protest. She simply turned up the volume and stared at the television with eyes welled up. Yes, she was choking! She was on the verge of apologizing. Almost there. I dilly-dallied to give her some time. A piece of paper with a half-torn envelope lay on the table. I picked it up to while away my time: it was the month's electricity bill. An instant shiver ran down my spine followed by a sudden urge to go pee. When I returned, she was still watching television: Alok Nath's 'Sandhi Sudha' advertisement for joint pain, can you believe it? That was what she was glued to at a time I was about to walk out on her.

Fine, I towed my suitcase out to the door, when I finally heard her call out.

'Yes?' I turned around expectantly.

'Make sure you shut the door properly on your way out!'

Fine! If that was what was meant to be, it would be. I got into my Santro, put the car in top gear (relative to the Santro's own capacity) and drove like an enraged maniac through the traffic. The Santro grunted angrily along with me. I had no idea where I was going. The first cheap, serviced apartment I could find, maybe. I found one twenty minutes later. It was as cheap as it could get, I gathered from the appearance.

'Rs 4,800 a night,' said the toothy manager at the reception. 'Rs 19,000 by the week.'

An hour later I returned to Mehek's apartment and quietly placed my suitcase in the living room. The electricity bill was missing from the table. Had she paid it already? *Fingers crossed!* I then tiptoed into the bedroom where she seemed to be sleeping very peacefully, not in the least perturbed that I had walked out on her. I snuggled up to her and whispered how much I loved her and that I had reversed my decision of putting up at *Heavenly Serviced apartments* because I knew how much we both had tried to keep this relationship going and both of us certainly deserved better than this childish behaviour. Without opening her eyes, she quietly said that she wanted to sleep. Sure, I said, if she could just let me know where she had kept the electricity bill…

'I have paid it,' she said with a slight sniffle. 'Don't worry about it now.'

Yay! Now I could sleep comfortably too. I needed this sleep. The event was a week away and I was losing whatever was left of my mind.

19
Baba Bhai

I AM NOT sure what time it must have been when the doorbell rang. I could hear Mehek in the shower, so I groggily dragged my feet out of the bedroom and into the living hall, where the maid had stopped mopping the floor and was staring in horror at my pink boxers. Exactly how many more times did I need to remind Mehek she must sound me off when the maid had already arrived? I stared at the maid, half-expecting her to open the door. She stayed on her haunches and stared at me in return. By now the doorbell had rung for the fourth time. Mehek had stepped out of the shower, her crimson towel wrapped over her petite head like a turban, beads of water kissing her eyelashes—God, she looked gorgeous. Ok, not so much when she snubbed me with 'Is that door going to open on its own or what?' I trudged up to the door and peeped through the eyehole in the door with the open eye. I saw what looked like a thick, grey shoelace.

Why was a shoelace dangling mid-air outside our door? I

tried focusing, but was reminded of those horrible days in the biology lab at school when I would be asked to observe the dissection of a sunflower leaf under the microscope—I could see nothing. I rubbed my eyes and focused again. It could have been a cat's whiskers. Then, some noise outside the door. Irritated, disturbed sounds. The whiskers moved back a little. Two diaphragms appeared right above the whiskers, expanding and contracting furiou...

Holy shit! I retreated, turned and ran as fast as I could. Behind me I could hear the doorbell ring again. I vaguely recall Mehek and the maid in the passage, looking at me as I made a dash for the French window. I also vaguely recall the maid scream 'BABA BHAI!' as I leapt out of the window from Mehek's eighteenth-floor deluxe apartment.

Before anyone makes irresponsible inferences about the weakness of my character, it is imperative you understand how the past week panned out. After that brief skirmish with Mehek when I realized I could not live a day without her—for the emotional anchoring and because I could not afford to rent a place in this goddamn city independently—I had given some serious consideration to her suggestion that I start fending for myself.

I had approached a recruitment consultant, albeit reluctantly, and projected myself as a writer-for-hire. She asked me to send my profile on a single page. That was not a problem at all because my accomplishments as a writer would not require more than a page of description. Just to be safe and also because I was psyching out, I prepared an alternate profile tailored to my once glorious consulting career and alongside floated this profile to a recruitment consultant in the business consulting space. Because, you know, two birds in the bush are a more exciting prospect than going hungry for the day.

While I waited for the consultants to call me back, the PR agents informed me that they had set me up for a pre-event interview with *Express News* the same afternoon. Delirious with joy and anticipation, I drove to the newspaper's head office an hour earlier and parked myself before the receptionist. Three hours later I was directed inside to Nandini, a journalist who looked like she had been placed there only to unnerve and insult me. She pointed towards two vacant chairs. I sat on one.

I began by introducing myself as the next boy wonder on the block, and a former miracle executive at Byte. Before I could finish she was shaking her head dismissively, gesturing to ask me for a copy of the book. Wait. She wanted a copy? Why was I not told this before? By this time she was looking at me as though I was wasting her valuable time because she had to catch the next flight to Tibet to interview the lamas there. I tried massaging her ego; of course I should have brought the book along, not a problem, I would run back and get it. She closed her eyes and pointed towards the exit. 'Make it quick.'

So I drove back home and returned a half hour later with one of the complementary copies I had received from Swarup. I was directed to her office. As I entered, her back was to me. She was perched on her chair with her feet resting on an open window sill, leisurely drinking a cup of coffee and staring at the nothingness outside. As soon as she heard me however, she shook her head.' Sorry. You're late,' she said stiffly. 'Come next week.'

I don't know what her problem was. But even Chirayu, the lowest class in the corporate species, had never been so ill-mannered. I argued that she did not look particularly busy and I didn't think it would hurt if she gave me an audience for ten minutes.

'Leave your book here, I will see what I can do,' she said. 'And may I ask you not to advise me on how much free time I have on hand?'

I had played the politeness card and it had failed. So I decided it was time I showed her what I really thought of her. I gave her a little homily on what I thought of her obnoxious behaviour and then reminded her for another ten minutes that she was not doing me a fucking favour by interviewing me —this was a *paid* interview the PR had set me up for. She listened to me in rapt attention, looked horrified and humiliated and then recovering from the shock, toned down a little and told me she would have something published in the papers very soon. I gave her a cold glance as I got up. This could have been so much easier had she not awoken the animal inside me.

One problem dealt with, I returned home to receive a call from one of the recruitment consultants. The excitement in her voice made my heart beat like a drum. Yes, there was a job opportunity she wanted me to apply to!

'What?' I asked her excitedly.

'A Verbal Ability lecturer at Passionate MBA Coaching Centre!'

Phuss. I felt like a pricked balloon. I told her there was no way on earth I was going to take up the job of a teacher. For one, I had never been particularly polite to my own teachers as a student and I feared karma would come and bite me in the ass. Secondly, I was not interested in coaching students to aspire to anything that resembled an MBA. The degree was over-rated, it got you jobs that often had nothing to do with what you studied in the course, and it filled you with unnecessary arrogance that prompted you to quit your job thinking you could conquer the bloody world with a story made of some random musings. No, I would not compromise on my ideals by teaching at an MBA centre.

A few more weeks without a job could not be any more significantly devastating. Maybe I could give Raghav another chance at redeeming his scruples. I called him everyday again that entire week—no response yet. One night before going to bed I called him from Mehek's mobile and posed as Nancy from an imaginary bank who wanted to sell him a home loan.

'Of course,' he said. 'Why don't we meet at the Hyatt for some sushi and ...'

'Great idea, son of a bitch,' I said, removing my handkerchief from the mouthpiece. 'Maybe then you could also return me my money.'

He hung up on me again.

Ok, coming back to my leap from the eighteenth floor French window of Mehek's apartment. I can still faintly recall the maid's scream—'BABA BHAI!'—as I leapt out of the window.

A word of caution. Please do not try this at home, at the Petronas towers, or anywhere else for that matter. Because jumping off a high-rise building is foolish and unforgivable. My case was a little different, because as I have stated often before, I am the kind of person who will not even yawn without having conducted a prior feasibility study. Yes, in rare cases my strategy has not quite paid off but, believe it or not, this thing about jumping off the window was well thought out.

Basically, while vegetating idly day after day in Mehek's living room, I had unintentionally ended up doing a little survey of what her building looked like. Two giant barrel-shaped towers, separated by a glass-shielded walkway; a giant window with a handlebar located on every floor of this walkway, with a small parapet jutting out of each window. To the average Joe this might be uninteresting, even ridiculously detailed, trivia. But I have always been a keen student of mathematics and applied logic, as would be evident if you'd ever get a chance to look at my CAT scorecard. And to my geeky mind this was a fascinating case study of the application of the laws of trigonometry.

It was occasions like these, when Mehek was on her way to open the door to her parents, that my mind did the math faster than Chacha Chaudhary's mind smelt ammunition. Mehek's French window was at an approximate distance of ten horizontal feet from the closest window of the walkway. This window was around eight feet below our balcony. I had to cover a parabolic distance of approximately thirteen feet to break into the walkway through that giant window.

My body of 88 kilos (mostly bone density, not too much fat FYI) had a lead pace of 15 kilometres an hour from Mehek's door. Considering the westerly winds blew at around 10 kilometres an hour at that altitude, I was well poised. The strategy was simple: I would execute the perfect parabolic jump, land on the parapet outside the window, open the handlebar and sneak into the walkway, out of sight before her parents could even get a whiff of who was inside the house.

I ran. I jumped. I conked my head against the window of the walkway. The rest of the incident is a blur, but our maid reconstructed some of it when I saw through that day and then we all talked about it and then everyone except me laughed over it. So, as the maid puts it rather dramatically, the doorbell had rung a gazillion times before I had even reached the French window. Because she had no idea what exactly I was up to, Mehek had proceeded to open the door and had missed the entire stunt I had executed in the meantime. By the time she got to the French window with her parents peeping behind her, I was perched somewhere near the window with my back facing my to-be in-laws. The collar of my shirt had got stuck in the handlebar, my right leg was on the parapet outside the window. My left leg was suspended freely like a waving flag, and it caught the attention of the security guard at the main gate—who otherwise keeps sleeping, that bugger.

'Thief, thief!' he shouted hurling his baton, a random piece of cloth and some abuses at me in quick succession. I could not afford to react because my attention was solely focused on getting my collar off that stubborn mule of a handlebar while ensuring my right leg did not move. During this time Daddy Gupta had heard the word 'thief', which placed his policing hormones on slow boil. He leaned out of the French window, pulled out a revolver and ordered me to surrender. Even in that tense, precarious moment the stupidity of that order was not lost on me. Bloody, my collar is stuck on the handlebar, I am almost nearly dead—how much more do you want me to surrender?

Did he want me to raise my hands in the air and close the file once and for all? Nonsense.

Mehek just stood there, frozen, ashamed and very, very scared.

Luckily the maid turned out to be my guardian angel.

'Do not shoot,' she squealed. 'This is not a thief, this is BABA BHAI!'

'BABA BHAI who?' Daddy Gupta growled, taking aim at my pink boxers. 'Your building cleaner, Mehek?'

Mehek was now dizzy from all the action. Her eyes began to drop. She held her head painfully and then slowly fainted into Mummy Gupta's trembling arms. This was something I needed an explanation for. I was the one dangling from the eighteenth floor of her building just to keep my word—that her parents must not discover that I had quit my job and was wasting away in her luxury apartment. And now when her father had pointed a pistol at me, she had conveniently passed out.

'Not the building cleaner,' the maid continued nervously. 'The BABA BHAI who stays here with DIDI!'

Merry Mayhem happened soon after. I somehow managed to get my shirt off that handlebar which was the root of all our miseries that day. I regained my senses and tried exiting over to the other tower and then hopefully out of the building and if possible out of the city. But Supercop Gupta was still nimble and agile and he intercepted me in the stairway.

'Come home, we need to talk,' he said, glancing angrily at my clothes.

'It is not what you think,' I said. 'I had noticed this building needed its windows to be cleaned, and I was free today so…'

'That is very thoughtful of you,' he said, opening the door to our apartment. 'Let us discuss this act of benevolence in detail.'

When we entered, Mehek had recovered from her low blood pressure and was all ready in her black designer blazer and skirt to leave for work leaving me in this helpless, embarrassing condition with her shocked parents. I scampered inside, put some pants on, and came back outside to greet the to-be in-laws formally. By now a lot of purpose of being polite and cordial was lost, but I still had to try my best. So I made those customary remarks about what a pleasant surprise it was to find them here in the city.

To which Daddy Gupta replied, 'We came here to attend the event and to give you a surprise. It turns out we were in for a surprise ourselves.'

Mehek picked up her bag and prepared to leave. I led her into the kitchen.

'You can't leave me stranded like that. Do something!'

She shook her shoulder off my grip angrily. 'You have put us here. You are the genius. Go figure!'

'How is it my fault your parents have landed up like this unannounced?' I hissed.

'I don't know about today,' she retorted. 'But somewhere you are to blame for this entire chaos we are in. I just can't nail it right now.'

That was it. That was the second time that week she was reminding me of a mistake I had been reminding myself every day for over a year. I could feel it in my bones. She was going to dump me. Not only would that break my heart but that would also mean I would really need to go around scouting for an apartment and shelling out rent again. Fuck. And if there was indeed a chance she might reconsider her decision, her angry parents were totally going to drive her to the edge.

But first, I faced a more formidable situation—conversing with her parents for an entire day with a straight face. It was not long before Mummyji asked me why I had not got ready to leave for work yet. This was a good opportunity for me to just don some formal clothes and get the hell out of there. But I was growing a little tired of hiding this inconvenient truth from them. It had to come out in the open eventually. Now was just as good a time as any other.

'I quit Bytesphere long ago,' I said.

'To go where?' Mummyji asked. I saw mortal fear on her face as she expected an undesired answer.

It was coming anyway. 'Nowhere. To write a book.'

Daddy Gupta kept his cup of tea aside. 'That contract with those literary agents?'

'Yes.'

There was a sense of relief on their faces, which was going to get murdered very soon, because I added: 'Except that the contract with Brian never came through.'

'Then? This book?'

'Is being published by a newbie of some sort,' I said, staring out of the window with as much composure as I could muster.

Daddy Gupta had now clutched the cup of tea hard. I had a feeling he was going to aim it at me. 'What do you mean?'

'That deal with the literary agents did not work out. I do not have that contract of fifty thousand dollars any more.'

'Do you need some more tea?' Mummy Gupta asked her

husband in nervous excitement, hoping to change the subject.

'Why did it not work out?'

'They were using my talent for commercial gains.'

'And what exactly did you have in mind?'

'I wanted my work to be respected for its creativity.'

He held his head. 'I have a migraine. I must get some sleep.'

Getting up, he turned around and asked me if there was room for them to be accommodated in the apartment too.

'Oh absolutely,' I stuttered. 'In fact, it is all yours. I was going to move to a serviced apartment tomorrow anyway.'

'Well, we are grateful, what can we say?' he paused, and then added. 'Wait. Have you been putting up here because you could not afford rent on your own?'

I laughed heartily in an effort to dismiss the allegation. But he began to walk away. I called after him to explain that just in case he was wondering, Mehek and I slept in different rooms because our relationship was based on trust and friendship rather than on primal lust.

'Good thing you told me,' he hollered from the room inside. 'Now if you please, I must change my nappies.'

An extremely awkward afternoon followed. Mummy Gupta and I sat through it in the living room, not so much as making eye contact with each other. When I realized none of us could take the silence any more, I switched on the television. Both of us watched *Sasuraal Simar Ka* for some time. During the course of this episode, we bonded a lot. Mummyji asked me about my daily routine. I told her I chatted a little with Mehek every morning after waking up (in a separate room); then we would breakfast together and once she left for work I watched television.

'This, *Sasuraal Simar Ka?*' she asked, slightly horrified.

'No, other shows too,' I cited *Saajan Saath Nibhaana, Des Mein Nikla Hoga Chaand* and was just about to mention *Anaamika* when she increased the volume of the television to indicate I must stop speaking. I was sensitive to the possibility that she had never envisioned a son-in-law who would watch television soaps at home. So I clarified it was all because I had just landed a contract for a month with a television channel to write dialogues for a few episodes of one of their flagship shows. And I had been asked to start following television soaps so I could understand the kind of tripe that was shown on them and what appealed to our audiences in general. The show sucked but they paid me an amount I was too embarrassed to disclose to her. If I made it past five episodes with quality dialogues, I could become a regular employee at their production house earning up to ten thousand an episode.

All of a sudden I found newfound respect in Mummyji's eyes. She looked at me, star struck, and then asked me if I knew Sakshi Talwar, and what did she look like in real life? I did not know who this girl was, but I entertained my mother-in-law to-be by telling her Sakshi looked ravishing and I could also tell from the few coffees I had had with her that she was very humble and had not let her success get to her head. Mummy Gupta was thrilled. She offered to help me make a deeper dive into the psyche of the soap watcher. I told her I had got a good grasp on most shows that mattered but was still trying to get hold of *Sasuraal Simar Ka*.

Fifteen minutes later, Daddy Gupta brought his sleepy head out of the bedroom into the living room. And what does he see?

His wife is explaining to me that Simar is upset with Siddhant because he bought her a very expensive salwar suit. I am sitting cross-legged on the couch and lapping up the details with great interest.

He held his head again with a moan and went back into the bedroom.

All of us heaved a sigh of relief when Mehek returned home and suggested we all walk down to Bandstand for a little stroll. That was a brilliant idea. A breath of fresh air could potentially work some magic in resolving this friction that everyone seemed to be developing with me.

'We are game, you tell us if you are up to it,' Daddy Gupta told her. 'We have all been resting all day. You are the only one who had some work.'

She whispered something angrily to her father, who turned away meekly and made no more sly remarks, at least for an hour. He spent an eternity ironing his Polo t-shirt before his wife reminded him we were going for a stroll and not an officers' club dinner.

After what her father had made me feel like, even the darkness of the Arabian Sea was very welcoming. We bought us some corn on the cob and proceeded to settle on the rocks by the shore.

'Why do we need to sit there?' Daddy Gupta protested. 'Let me call the police station and ask them to send some folding chairs…'

Mehek shushed him and led us all to the rocks. After a bit of grumbling, he asked her how her day had been. In a twist of fate, her company had chosen that very wretched day to announce her promotion to the role of senior advisory something-difficult-to-spell. I did not even need to imagine where the rest of this family conversation was heading now. Now you must know that I have always been an utterly selfless, uncompetitive man who only believes in excelling at his own work without making flimsy comparisons but what the hell was going on really. I loved Mehek. I loved to see her do well but it was not all that exciting to see her do better than me because that just spoiled the entire equation of our love by making me insanely jealous and insecure. However, because I am the liberal twenty-first century man I screamed in excitement and congratulated her, to which she said, 'It is not such a big deal also.'

Yeah, right. Humility + Excellence = best daughter ever tied to a good-for-nothing wannabe. Of all the time she had spent in the company, they had to choose that very day to promote her. Mummyji was very thrilled and offered to cook us kheer after dinner.

'Actually, Nakul likes orange soufflé more,' she said, 'I was wondering if we could buy some jelly...'

'But *you* like kheer,' Daddy Gupta interjected. 'Who got the promotion, everyone? Kheer it will be.'

'I need to take a walk,' I got up and walked away. I could do with being a little away from the sarcasm. I had an interview the next day to focus my energies on. When I returned hours later, the father and daughter were in animated conversation while the mother was nervously murmuring something to herself —I think she was chanting the Hanuman Chalisa. The whispered discussion ended abruptly when Daddy Gupta saw me towering over him.

'Come, we were just talking about you,' he said.

'I know,' I said, sitting down a few feet away. 'Mehek, can I have a word with your father for a bit?'

Mehek was startled, of course, but it was so heart-warming to see the colour drain off Daddy Gupta's face. He cowered like a terrified baby on one corner of the rock, looking at me, perplexed. Mehek and her mother went on a long walk, after which I began asking him what exactly his problem was and what I could do to alleviate it. He said he had no problem and was very proud of me (this was said with zero conviction), but he worried about a future that was not hedged (Mehek had taught him this word too?) against a volatile economy. Now that the gloves were already off, I brought in a purposeful, sharp reference to Sameer Kashyap—apparently when that first class show-off quit his job at the same company and went off with a band of gypsies on some bullshit mountaineering expedition that added no value to either himself or to our volatile economy, Daddy Gupta had been very impressed with him. And at the end of the entire drama, what had he made for himself? A couple of yoga ashrams in some obscure corners of the world.

'I have a bigger dream than those yoga ashrams,' I said defiantly.

'Yes, only that he monetized his dream,' said Daddy Gupta, and then added. 'Look, I do not mean to put you down. I only care for you.'

In the holy name of Jesus Christ! This was his way of caring for me! I was so overwhelmed you might think those waves below the rocks were spouting out of my eyes. And just because he had brought up monetizing, I slipped in the news of my contract for writing the channel's new show *Teri Aankhon Mein Dekha Maine Ek Nanha Sapna*. He looked at me crestfallen, probably imagining how he would introduce me in front of his fellow officers in the fraternity.

'At least it will monetize,' I smiled, reading his mind.

On that note, we joined Mehek and Mummyji on the walk back home. I asked to take leave of them so I could go check in to my service apartment.

'Oh, let it be, just stay with us,' Daddy Gupta said stubbornly.

'Like I said, Mehek and I sleep in two different rooms,' I said, 'so we are going to be cramped for space.'

'How nice, isn't it?' he said. 'In that case, let Mehek sleep with her mother. And if you don't mind, you could give me some space on your bed?'

Good God. Tonight was so not going to be a good night. Mehek looked mortified.

'Nakul talks in his sleep sometimes,' she blurted out.

'How do you know?' Mummy Gupta asked her shamefacedly.

'He told me,' she said.

'How do you know you talk in your sleep?' Daddy Gupta turned to me.

'Guys, let's just go home,' I pleaded. 'I have an important day ahead of me.'

20
....
Hair We Are

I ARRIVE AT *the decrepit office of the publisher. A sign outside the door reads 'If you have been here before and have been turned down, please leave now.' I try to remember. I don't think I have been here before, although I have been to scores of other offices all day. I have now disowned my body odour because I am too ashamed of the way I smell.*

'Here, take this,' the receptionist offers me her perfume. I dab some thankfully and settle down on the couch.

She flips through the spiral bound manuscript I have handed her and lets out a little smirk. 'Will you have some tea?'

She adds, before I can respond. 'There is soufflé but we do not offer it to strugglers usually.'

A cup of tea arrives, cold as an ice-cream and laden with a kilogram of cream. I nearly vomit after lapping it up in one gulp. I ask the receptionist if I can now see the publisher—I have been waiting on that couch since the time that tea was first boiled on the kettle. Just then a door opens. Sameer Kashyap walks out and beckons me with a snap of his finger, to follow him. I pick up the manuscript from the receptionist's desk and nearly hurl it at the bastard, but check myself just in time.

Inside his cabin (the self-obsessed loser has a portrait of himself in there), he opens my manuscript, looks at it disdainfully and then throws it in the trash can.

'Sorry, it cannot be monetized.'

I clutch his arms in an earnest plea. 'Please don't say that. You are my last hope.'

'Like I said, this is not happening,' he repeats in that fake, calm, Raymond manner, and gets up to leave.

I grab the end of his suit, but he shakes me off. I hold his hand, but he tries to drag his body away. I finally hold him by the hair, pin him down to his table, and plead again.

He screams in pain. 'Let go of my hair. That hurts!'

'I won't let go. Please give me a chance,' I am now in tears.

'I SAID LET GO OF MY HAIR!' he screams.

He screams so loudly that I wake up.

It must have been around the break of dawn. Under the dim blue light of the sky outside, I saw I had held Daddy Gupta by his silky, brown hair. His head was firmly gripped under my hands, but his body was wriggling and writhing in pain. His larynx was on fire as he continued screaming, 'Let go of my hair!'

Two watery eyes stared at me in the blue darkness minutes after I had let go. It was an awkward moment to strike a conversation, but I still managed to mutter, 'Good morning Papa.' Then he sprang out of bed and ran out of the room, shouting and creating unnecessary drama.

'He tried to assault me!' he kept screaming until Mehek and Mummyji ran out of their room. 'IPC 351, IPC 351!'

The lights were switched on. His shirt was drenched in sweat and his hair looked like a DNA double helix drawn by a drunk biology student. I fetched him a glass of water from the kitchen and offered it to him.

He looked at the glass with mortal fear. '*You* drink it first. Here, in front of all of us!'

'Come on, Dad,' Mehek grunted in dismay while casting one nasty glance at me. So now seeing a vivid dream in my sleep was also a crime I would be tried for. I tried pacifying him but he was too tormented for words. He walked over to the mirror in the foyer to examine his hair and face—God knows, maybe looking for torture marks. In an effort to lighten up the mood in the house, I offered to cook everyone omelettes for breakfast. But on Daddy Gupta's cue, Mummyji came sprinting behind me and insisted she would do all the cooking and that I should just…go sit in a corner and…do my thing.

Even I was fed up of trying to win these difficult people over. I would rather just leave them and get out somewhere to get some alone time and mentally prepare myself for the event in the evening. I went in for a shower and found my tube of shaving cream lying next to Daddy Gupta's toothbrush in the toothbrush holder. I had good reason to believe he had brushed his teeth with my shaving cream, but given that he had already concluded I was out to harm him I decided to keep my mouth shut about it and let him continue using it if he had liked the taste. When I emerged from the shower, Mehek crept into the room and conveyed something with her hand gestures, which could be classified either as a string of abuses or a very serious threat.

I put on my best available pair of jeans and my best available t-shirt, got a satchel out of an old collection so that I could look like a sincere writer, and stepped out into the hall, all set to leave. Then, only because I realized I had a moral and a social obligation towards them and partly because of Mehek's threat, I asked Daddy and Mummyji if they would like me to take them out somewhere shopping after they had finished breakfast. Both of them vehemently declined the offer and said they felt very nice and cosy at home. I turned to my left and saw Mehek give me the glare again.

I thought it best to just leave. Mehek saw me off to the elevator. I asked her if I could pick the parents up from home later and drive them to the event, but she said they were too emotionally fragile at that time to be willing to sit in my Santro and that she would have her car sent to pick them up in the evening. I shrugged; that suited me alright. She kissed me good luck and sent me on my way.

I was running out of luck already. I started the car and saw I was nearly out of fuel. I took a brief digression, refuelled the vehicle, and drove on for fifteen minutes to find I was out of fuel again. I called Gopi to ask him details about the fucking mystery of the fuel tank of this piece of trash he had handed me. He said there was absolutely nothing wrong with the fuel tank; only the fuel needle sometimes failed to behave itself and jiggled its way down to the zero mark even on a full tank. But he assured me that was only a small obstacle because I only needed to play safe by making a trip to the petrol pump every alternate day, 'just to make sure you are never out of fuel.'

Bastard Gopi. I would ask Mehek to report him to Goldman Sachs and get him stripped off all those corporate deals he was lackeying. For the time being I found myself a quiet corner in the same old café and rehearsed my speech over and over again. A couple seated at a table a few feet away began staring at me with pity. They thought I was crazy and mumbling to myself. I smiled at them and said everything was fine and there was nothing exciting for them to be involved in. But their curiosity got the better of them and they started talking to me much against my wishes. I did not want to be rude, so I entertained them for a short while. They said they had noticed me seated at the same corner table often over the last year and were always curious what I did all day long sitting at the table sporting worn-out shorts and a scraggly beard. I felt elated for a fleeting moment—someone, after all, had noted what I had been up to all year with so much interest.

'I write,' I said with a proud smile.

They looked at me blankly and then said, 'That is ok. But what do you do?'

What nonsense did that mean?

'I write!' I replied more firmly.

The man clucked his tongue. This answer just did not work for him. 'No, no. All that is fine. Everyone writes. What do you do for a living?'

I wanted to say I used to be a consultant. I earned twenty lakh a year, plus some fat bonuses. I had a snazzy car, membership with Hilton Honors, and was the envy of all my batchmates. Then I quit my job to write. I had not earned a single penny in the last thirteen months and had a new assignment that might or might not pay me anything either; and close with, 'Now, do you want to adopt me or something?'

But for want of time, I simply said that I was a novelist waiting for my first book to release and hoped it would be received well enough for me to never go back to a job again. They gave me that same look of pity again. The man marched to the billing counter and told the manager that my coffee was on him. His wife smiled at me and said they were very rich investors of some kind and felt very moved by my story and treating me to a coffee was the least they could do for me.

I looked at her coldly and then added. 'Actually, I am also very hungry because I have not eaten anything since morning.'

'Of course, of course,' she said before signalling to her investor husband to buy me two submarine sandwiches.

There, my lunch was sorted. I took the sandwiches, thanked them and left, never to return to that café.

~

I was the first person to reach the bookstore. The manager greeted me warmly and assured me that all arrangements were in place. I took a quick look; a table with three chairs—one each for the author, the chief guest, and the manager of the bookstore, and fifty chairs facing the table and placed in a neat matrix. I looked at the manager a little unhappily and said we could do with a few more chairs—press invites had gone out to a large number of journalists, and at least two hundred friends had written to me on Facebook that they would be present at the occasion. The manager said it was a Friday evening and he did not think we would need a fifty-first chair, when a voice boomed from behind him.

'Don't worry. If he cannot bring you the chairs, we will organize them from somewhere.' We turned to see Mr Rao and Mr Kamdar in their crisp uniforms, towering ominously over the now terrified manager.

'Of course I can organize them, but…' the manager attempted to reason.

'Then please do,' said Mr Kamdar. And there that discussion ended.

I took a stroll around the store as I waited for Mehek and her parents to arrive. I examined the standee next to the table rack where a hundred copies of my book had been displayed.

Crossways invites you to the launch of Nikhil Kapoor's 'The Chaos Project', this evening, 5.00 p.m.

Ok, very impressive, except that they had got my first name wrong. The manager apologized profusely, took out a pen to scratch out 'Nikhil', and overwrote 'Nakul' on it.

'No one will notice,' he grinned.

Of course. Anyway, I turned my attention to the few customers who had begun to stream into the store. I waited fifteen minutes and watched covertly. Only one Chinese tourist had picked up my book so far and had then walked away to the gadgets' section at the far end—no surprises as far as his choices were concerned. Just then, a young boy whom I was going to start hating in about a hundred seconds, looked at the spiral structure in awe. He picked up a copy, read the blurb on the back cover, and wailed so shrilly he almost shattered his mother's reading glasses. Then he angrily flung the copy like a Frisbee and narrowly missed knocking the emcee of the event down. Seconds later, the beautiful spiral, so elegantly built with copies of my labour of love, came crashing and became a debris-pile, the way my dreams had so often in the year gone by.

'I don't want shitty books, I want Superman!' He wailed. His mother looked at the staff, half-confused, half-apologetic. I walked up to the boy and ruffled his hair lovingly. In my mind, of course, I yanked the hair off his head rather violently. But given that I was geared up for an important occasion, I down played my inner feelings and bought him a cheap Superman toy from the shelf. His mother started the customary 'Oh, this was not necessary' drama. I gave her the 'Read between the lines, lady!' look. She looked at the debris being reassembled by the staff. Reluctantly, she picked up a copy, paid up, and then dragged her jubilant boy out of the store.

When Mehek finally walked in with her parents, exactly two customers had taken their seats in the audience, wondering what the event was all about. Apparently, Daddy Gupta had received strict instructions from Mehek to be nice and sensitive towards me and to avoid saying anything that ruptured my self-esteem.

So he looked at the rows of empty chairs and turned to me, smiling. 'Nice ambience! Shall we begin?' This was the best he could have come up with, I had to give it to him. I motioned towards the chairs so they could all settle down.

Meanwhile the grand total of three journalists with cameramen, who had turned up to cover my event, were now getting crabby. They wanted to leave; the chief guest was nowhere in sight yet, and neither were the snacks promised in the press invite. I pleaded with them to wait. Ok, but only for half an hour, they declared, as though their newspapers would shut down in their absence.

Apparently, Mallika Sherawat was returning to India and they needed to go cover her (not literally, one of them said and laughed alone). I suggested maybe I had also called someone worth covering and they suddenly started prodding me to disclose the name of the chief guest. I tried skirting the discussion, but the overenthusiastic emcee came beaming before them and screamed like a mad fan girl, 'DINO MOREA!' Whatever little patience the journalists had left, now quite properly disappeared. They got upset with me for sending an exaggerated press note that mentioned 'surprise celebrity and media magnet will preside…'

This was so annoying. I spent the next ten minutes explaining myself to them: How I had initially approached Shahrukh Khan's office and his receptionist had said 'Sir would charge twenty-five lakhs for the appearance.' I explained he only had to come snip a ribbon off the book, I was not asking him to purchase the bookstore. Unfortunately the deal didn't work out because the receptionist started behaving like she was Shahrukh herself. Someone told me to approach Dino Morea instead, because he was very humble and mostly very free also. His business manager confirmed that Dino would surely come, in fact he might bring along some like-minded friends from the industry for added media pull.

Having reeled off my saga I looked at them expectantly and was not disappointed. After some bickering, we came to an agreement: the photographers would quickly do a small photo-op with me and then leave for the airport to take pictures of Mallika Sherawat. The scribes stayed back because they conceded they had the same questions to ask her that they did two years ago, and agreed they could dig them out from archives.

People had started pouring in. Some had taken their seats before the podium and were getting a little restless. Mehek suggested I begin the event without Dino Morea. I was about to start howling my lungs out when Dino's business manager asked me to come to the gate. I rushed out excitedly with Mehek following me; a sedan pulled over and a fat, bald, middle-aged, sweaty man walked out and waved at me. The sedan drove away. Frankly, I had never seen a Dino Morea movie but I didn't think that was what he looked like. Mehek confirmed my suspicions. The bald man came and introduced himself as Dino Morea's business manager.

'Sir has got into a very tight gym regime for his new look in a superhero film,' the business manager explained, 'so he is very tired. He has sent me to cut your ribbon instead.'

I had tears in my eyes now, not so much because of Dino's no-show as by this egghead trying to hog the limelight at the event. He was supposed to launch my book, then shut up and sit down in a corner and let me read paragraphs from the novel. Instead, he started drawing parallels between Dino's early struggle and my early reckoning in the field of literature. If I had abs like a hero's, I wouldn't be sobbing about 'struggles'. At least thrice he mentioned I would need to work very hard to be successful like Dino Morea. I was about to slap him now. Thankfully, he concluded his speech by handing me a rolled-up sheet decorated with a pink ribbon.

'A memo from Dino Sir,' he announced as I unravelled the

sheet. The cameramen leaped forward to take pictures.

It turned out to be a poster of Dino Morea wearing nothing but leather pants. Below was a message,

'To the author it may concern: Love, luck and XOXO – Dino.'

By now I had lost context of what this event was all about. The emcee reminded me, and so prompted I read out excerpts from my book. Daddy Gupta saw the disappointment on my face even as he scanned the empty rows of chairs in the audience. He gestured to Mr Kamdar who went scuttling across the store to catch hold of customers and deposit them on the empty chairs. He caught hold of the Chinese tourist who was now just about to leave the store, apparently demanding to see his passport, which the tourist was clearly not carrying with him. 'Big punishment!' Mr Kamdar rolled his eyes at the petrified tourist. 'Ok, sit for the event. I let you go.'

A few more additions to the nearly disinterested audience. I continued reading. Customary applause. Staccato yawns escaped pursed mouths. From the crowd, an odd whisper: 'Every-bloody-body is becoming an author now.' I was about to throw the microphone in the direction of that voice, but was held back by a sudden question that wound me back to when it all started.

'What prompted you to be a writer?'

Wow. That felt like a long time ago. I stared at the blank wall at the far end of the hall. The bored audience stared back at me, confused and frustrated with my silence. My mind panned out of the emcee's prompts, the hushed whispers in the crowd, and the embarrassed look on Mehek's and her parents' faces. Dino's business manager was busy with his phone, possibly texting Dino that he did a good thing by not attending this lacklustre event. I had felt it in my bones that this might not turn out to be a grand affair. But I had not anticipated this.

I zoned out. In front of everyone. It was all over.

21

Rating: Not Applicable

So, THINGS HAD turned out a little better than I had feared. Of course, the media was as ruthless as I had anticipated, but at least they gave me *some* coverage in the papers. Even if it was just a picture of me staring at a wall with an expression that suggested I was on dope, with the following piece below:

Dino Morea gifts topless picture to struggling author

In a grandiose gesture, actor Dino Morea gifted a large pin-up poster of himself in leather pants to a fan who launched his debut novel at a city bookstore last evening. The author apparently went into a stupor on seeing the poster. It is reckoned that Morea's new superhero film has some fans in a trance already and it might just turn out to be a new trendsetter in cinema.

Despite this piece of shit in the papers, I had managed to garner readers. My work was finally getting traction. Customers had indeed bothered to pick up my book, read it, and email me feedback. I was touched already. The tone of their responses made me feel even more alive. The old Nakul Kapoor was back—the man his industry loved back, the man who rose against all odds (such as regular intervention by his parents and in-laws who did not believe that writing episodes of *Teri Aankhon Mein Dekha Maine Ek Nanha Sapna* was a real job, and the man who was now a degree less insecure about his girlfriend's recent promotion to the post of senior advisory something).

Mehek had been very worried lately about my bleak future and was particularly upset with the low turnout at my book launch and with what her father had to say about the low turnout. Now with the readers writing in, I told her we had two reasons to celebrate, not just her promotion. And this time the treat would be on me, soon as I returned from my seven-city tour of book reading events. She looked at me, mortified, and asked me if these events were worth my (remaining) money. I did not like the tone in her voice, but I tried being nice to her. I ran her through the vast number of emails I had been getting from my fans—one of them had even threatened to write me a letter in blood if I did not meet him at Café Coffee Day the next morning.

My PR team thought I needed to cash in on this early frenzy I had created following the launch of my event and let my book make waves in other cities as well. Of course, threats of blood-soaked letters were not the only kind of email I had received. There were some smart asses who would write to abuse me, not necessarily because they had read the book and had hated it, but possibly also because they had not found anyone else to abuse all day. I was particularly ticked off by a guy studying in some engineering college, apparently some sort of a geek—who claimed that all the comments and ratings on my book on all online stores were fabricated by me and that he could prove it by finding out all the IP addresses from where the reviews were posted. I told the useless, desperate fucker to vent out the frustration of his engineering exams on someone else because I did not care two hoots. Then I sent him another email saying I had close to a 1 GB collection of high definition Sweet Sinner videos and was wondering if anyone from his institute would be willing to take them from me for absolutely free? After some further exchange of emails the issue of these IP addresses was amicably sorted.

But Mehek still thought visiting cities for these events would be wasting a lot of money on flights and that I would rather take the passive approach of begging of people on the social network to buy my book. I did not blame her. Someone like her who had not journeyed the long road from clueless struggle to being inundated by fan mail would not see much sense in what I did. But I knew better than to persuade the same friends who had vanished from the face of the earth during my struggle, to now go and buy my book. No. I would take the market by storm like a man. Face to face, in bookstores, answering tough questions, braving the media, and most importantly—not inviting any celebrities. I was still in the process of persuading her about my decision when one evening I overheard Daddy Gupta ask her on Skype if she had paid for my tickets.

Alright, I was so done. I was going on this multi-city tour at my own expense. Ok, I paid for the tickets with the joint credit card I held with Mehek (who was the primary owner), but I would pay her the day my first royalty cheque reached me.

The tour was fun, except for some ridiculous conversations that took place in a couple of them. For example, a girl at the Kolkata event insisted on knowing why I had put up a much younger picture of myself on the book jacket, when in reality, 'you look like this!' But such anomalies were well made up for by the long queues of eager readers who lined up to get their copies autographed by me. By the time I was headed back to Mumbai, I had made news headlines in some newspaper supplements at least.

I met one such reader on the flight back home. They were now beginning to recognize me at public places. Maybe I would need to consider more covert appearances eventually, because I don't think Mehek would appreciate so much bonhomie.

'Have you written *The Chaos Project*?' he asked, wide-eyed.

I asked him to repeat the question a little louder so that I (and everyone else in the aircraft) could hear him a little better. He obliged. I nodded with a broad, exaggerated smile; yes indeed, I was the guy who...

'Your book is crap, bro.' He handed me a newspaper.

Bloody moron. I looked at him stunned. So did everyone else in the aircraft. I unrolled the newspaper to read the headline on page, I don't know, maybe 35 of the supplement:

Another newbie brings a dud to the Indian fiction market

I have even stopped wondering what comes over these new kids on the block who think that just because they can dabble in some sort of scribbling, they can get up and write a book and even have the gall to publish it. This trend is appalling. Nakul Kapoor, the latest in a series of such disappointments, comes up with something called 'The Chaos Project', which is another less-than-run-of-the-mill tripe sold in the name of a novel. It does not matter how much this book costs in the market. You will feel fleeced anyway. Avoid it like the plague.

Rating: Not applicable

I looked at the guy who had handed me this rubbish newspaper and smiled politely, saying criticism was an indispensable dark side to the aura that surrounded celebrated writers and that I just needed to take such news in my stride. Then I went to the toilet with the newspaper in my hand and cried my lungs, nerves and arteries out. When I regained my senses I turned to see the name of the newspaper: *Express News*.

Ah, I should have known. And then I noticed the name of the columnist: *Nandini Sreekar*.

Well played, Nandini. Well played.

When I landed, I had twelve missed calls from the television channel and an SMS from the content head that read: 'Urgent. Bad news. Call.'

Twelve missed calls were a hint big enough to know this was bad news. The shameless guys never called me twelve times to tell me what a scintillatingly beautiful episode I had written. Of course it was bad news. What was it, I called him and asked. He said I needed to come to their office immediately and kill off the lead character for the next episode.

'Why?' I asked, shocked.

'Budget constraints,' he replied. 'The show is not doing great. We will air two more episodes and call it a wrap. Sad end to the show. The hero dies. The heroine goes to offer penance in the mountains. We have it all sorted.'

'So what is the way ahead for me?' I asked part-nervously,

part-desperately.

'Keep in touch,' were his famous last words.

I did not inform Mehek about this wonderful development until the final episode had been written and submitted. I carried the cheque home and showed it to her with as much emotion and intensity as I could garner.

'The contract has ended,' I said, and on seeing the colour drain off her face, quickly added. 'But I have a lot of fight left in me.'

She undid her office blazer. Flinging it tiredly on the couch, she muttered before walking away towards the bathroom: 'Congratulations.'

22

Party on My Mind

SHIVANG APTE WROTE to me three months after I had emailed him: there was a note of apology for the delayed response and a request for my phone number. He called me soon as I responded to him, apologizing profusely for having missed reading my email because of the thousands of fan mails he used to get in response to his book every day. I assured him he did not have to apologize because I could myself relate to that overwhelming feeling of dealing with fan mails every living minute of my life; I was in fact contemplating hiring a secretary who could read and reply to every mail on my behalf.

(All of thirty-three emails had come my way since the release of my book three months ago. Twenty-nine of those emails were by the same fan, who could not stop asking me if I would be willing to co-author my next book with him. The last 'fan mail' I had received was at least fifty days ago).

Shivang was very surprised to hear I received fan mail too.

He said he did not even know I had written a book. There is nothing wrong in being truthful, I know, but I wanted to kill him when he said that. Instead I just dismissed the discussion saying it could possibly be so because of the low profile I kept and my dislike for interacting much with the media. Then he Googled me and said he just happened to read Nandini Sreekar's review of my book in the *Express News* and that he was very sorry for me. I replied it was great talking to him but I now needed to get back to writing my next book for which I would ideally like to preserve some self-esteem and motivation. Before hanging up he told me he was travelling to Mumbai towards the end of the month, because apparently Karan Johar had bought the film rights to his book and in a goodwill gesture had agreed to launch his book in front of the entire media at The Taj. Was this guy fucking kidding me? I Googled. No, he was damn serious. Karan Johar had indeed found something in his book which apparently no one had found in mine. Shivang asked me if I would be willing to meet him for a cup of coffee later the same night at The Taj because he was going to be put up there for the night by his publisher.

His publisher had him put up in a Taj suite. My publisher had stopped taking my calls; he now even recognized the number of the PCO booth from which I had started calling him to make queries about sales and royalties.

I told Shivang I would let him know after checking my schedule, which was actually nothing to check about because I no longer had a schedule. I had lost the only job I had, after obediently killing off the lead guy in the show. I now sat at home all day, writing when I could, ruminating when I could not, and deftly avoiding any kind of interaction with Mehek at all times that we were both home, except for the day she came up to inform me that Aniket had planned a celebratory party for her promotion at his house (what the fuck) and had insisted that she bring me along. This conversation apart, we were pretty much at that fragile stage of our relationship where I was confused whether I was supposed to hold on and make things work or I needed to move on and explore any available connections with Sagarika beyond the spiritual compatibility we felt with each other during those meditation one-on-ones. Because it would be utterly shameless and selfish on my part to call the dibs on this decision, I simply stoked Mehek for some time by routinely asking her, 'So where are we headed now that I am convinced I do not quite line up your alley?' to which she would say something as vague as 'There is no need to be dramatic' and then disappear again for the next twelve hours.

All this procrastination on a crucial decision had some very bad repercussions. Sagarika left the meditation academy and was replaced by a very rude, mannerless, mustachioed fellow called Parikshit Dabholkar who seemed to think he was singularly responsible for the creation of the seven chakras of life. He always stayed on extremes of either excessive boredom or unnecessary and exaggerated aggression. I could never understand how a man like him could help his students gain inner calm. On the second day of facing his arduous class I had tried getting up in the middle of his session to grab a glass of water, so that I could try my best to stay awake when he told us maybe for the fortieth time how he had conquered the desire to smoke cigarettes by tuning his mind to say 'no.'

'DO NOT TOUCH THAT WATER!' he screamed so loudly I sent the glass crashing to the floor in my nervousness. 'You do not really want it.'

'I do want it,' I insisted. 'I have just driven an hour in the heat to get here. I am sure I want it.'

'No, it is a distraction from your goal of attaining nirvana,' he bellowed, glared at me and ordered me to sit down.

Who the fuck was this man, seriously? Who told him I was there to attain nirvana? I just needed some peace of mind which he punctured daily by saying ridiculous things like, 'In our lives we take many pathetic decisions but that must not deter us from moving towards detachment because salvation is above all stupidity.' By the end of the first week I had safely concluded this guy had some trouble being happy in general and was here to vent it all out on us by treating this yoga class like a concentration camp. I asked the organizers of the meditation programme to refund the remainder of my fees; I did not need life advice from Parikshit Dabholkar. As I had feared, the fees were non-refundable and I just did not have the heart to waste all that money. So I attended the remaining sessions which proved sufficient for Dabholkar to completely destroy my mental stability. Once I had such an urge to go pee but was forced to sit through his entire session just so that I would not have to listen to some shit like 'Peeing is just a state of mind.'

And when he was not crazily aggressive, he was utterly boring. At the end of every class he asked us to close our eyes and focus on our navel because 'all the chakras of the body are concentrated in the navel' or something like that. One day he spoke so long about the life experiences his navel had taught him that I involuntarily drifted into sound sleep instead of focusing on the meditation. Half an hour later he heard me snore in the last row, and then humiliated me by yelling at me and asking me to leave the class.

I sought alternate sources of nirvana, such as walking randomly around a bookstore and sighing exaggeratedly on seeing my book still alive on the shelves, and nearly dying of excitement each time a customer even carelessly caressed it while walking past an aisle. A few days later, the visibility of the book started dwindling. It all felt like some sort of mirage. One store, then the other, then a third. MY BABY HAD BEEN DISOWNED BY THE STORES!

I decided to confirm with one of the store co-ordinators. He fed the name of the book into his computer and told me there were three copies in his store. So the good news was it had not been disowned. The bad news was those three copies were nowhere to be found. I ransacked all the shelves and nearly vandalized the store. No. I could not find them. He reluctantly joined me in the search. A lifetime later, he pulled out one copy that was stuck inside the pages of a cookbook in the 'Food and Drink's section'. The second copy was retrieved from debris of toys that had been put up for sale on the centre table. The third copy, he realized, was lying in the store room and they had forgotten to showcase it altogether. Looking at my distraught face, he tried explaining that they did not have enough room to showcase all books with equal visibility and hence sometimes the less successful ones had to bite the dust in the lower racks and thereby live a life of anonymity. I prayed he would stop his explanation right there. Instead, he offered me Shivang Apte's book and encouraged me to buy it instead of my own because, 'That book, *The Chaos Project*? That is a flop book, Sir.' Then he embarrassed me further by flipping open the jacket cover of *The Chaos Project* and turning red in the face on seeing my picture printed inside.

'Actually it is a very nice book,' he corrected himself, and then placated me a little by placing one copy right next to the front door. 'It is doing very well these days.'

'That is very nice to know,' I replied indifferently and asked him to tell me how much it had sold across all their outlets and how many more copies had been ordered by their distribution centre. He gave me the numbers with a very sad expression and added no further orders had been placed. I stormed out of the store and called Swarup, who explained he was more than happy to supply further orders if the stores were willing to purchase it. I went back inside the store. The store co-ordinator connected me on his phone to the chief manager in their head office, who said they were more than happy to buy more copies if Swarup could reduce the price; he was selling pedestrian fiction and not some Sachin Tendulkar memorabilia. I snapped at the store manager; whose work did he think he was calling pedestrian? And then I relayed the information back to Swarup who was still on the line. Swarup asked me to tell the store manager to mind his own business instead of telling him how to price his products. The store manager asked me to tell Swarup to stick to supplying the book to government libraries because that was all he was capable of doing.

'Oh you just tell him to shut up!' hissed Swarup.

'No you ask *him* to shut up!' bellowed the store manager.

I knew what I had to do. I hung up on both of them and walked out into the sunset.

I got the second recruitment agent to line me up for an interview for the role of a consultant in some firm whose name I had never heard. The job description sounded like something I could have done in my teens at a third of my current calibre. But this was all I needed to get my foot back in the door and then zip up the ranks and take the consulting industry by storm once again. The interview turned out to be some kind of a cheap joke. The panel was only interested in having me answer one question: 'Why did you have to leave your previous job?'

Bloody, I did not *have* to leave it, I left it because I wanted to. I answered at least three times in different ways such as, 'To rediscover myself,' 'To find the purpose of life,' or simply 'Because I needed a break'. Each response was received by a smirk—I do not know why it is so difficult for people to accept that people can aspire to a life outside of their office cubicles too. They stressed me out with the same question for so long that by the time they started asking me sensible questions about what I had done at Bytesphere, I had lost my focus and was once again found staring at the blank wall the way I had at the book launch.

They had too much attitude for a company of their scale and size. Maybe I just needed to try and find a route back into Bytesphere without getting, or at least sounding, desperate. So I waited for days at end until I finally found Chirayu online on Facebook at the unearthly hour of one in the night.

Nakul: Hi! How have you been?

Chirayu Consults: I was alright so far! And you?

Nakul: *The usual... things are great as always. Just thought of calling on you to check how things are back at work.*

Chirayu Consults: *Fantastic, Nakul. You have no idea how much things have changed in the last year. I got promoted to vice president and because the board considered that my competencies were not being adequately justified they also handed me the additional role of the interim head of finance. But these official roles apart, as a part of my moral obligation towards the company I still continue to hold my old post...*

[Approximately forty-five minutes later during which time I had completed two levels of Candy Crush Saga...]

Nakul: *It is wonderful to hear so much about Bytesphere once again. It feels like I am back in that office.*

Chirayu Consults: *Oh, sorry. Change the subject.*

Nakul: *No, not at all. I have been thinking a lot about all of you lately.*

Chirayu Consults: *Really? Why would you do that? Oh, by the way... I am sorry I could not make it to your event. But I saw a picture in the papers the next day. Were there just too many chairs put up there or had people generally not turned up?*

Nakul: *You jealous, insecure bastard. At least I had an event. What have you been doing all these years exc... [backspace, backspace, backspace]... Yeah, it would have been nice had you been able to come. So I was saying, I have been thinking a lot about you all lately.*

Chirayu Consults: *Why?*

Nakul: *Generally, I know I left a lacuna after my resignation. I hope my role has been filled up by someone worthy...*

Chirayu Consults: *Wait a minute, I just got a little emotional.*

Let me go wipe my tears...

Nakul: *Alright, sonofagun, that was probably the wittiest line you have come up with, I will give you that. Now if your fat ego has been satisfied...* [backspace, backspace, backspace]

Chirayu Consults: *Ahaaa, so that's what it is all about, old fellow? Why don't we get direct, huh? Do you want to come back? Out of things to do already?*

Nakul: *YOU POMPOUS PIG I WILL PLUCK OUT YOUR INNARDS IF YOU DO NOT STOP YOUR WISECRA...* [backspace, backspace]. *No Chirayu, I am quite comfortable. But I have enough experience now to handle a job alongside writing books, so I can surely consider coming back... only if you need me, of course.*

Chirayu Consults: *LOL.*

Nakul: *Well?*

And he went offline, the bastard. I should never even have broached the subject with him. I had first renounced my job. Now I had also renounced my pride.

Since there was nothing further to lose in life, I agreed to tag along with my hotshot girlfriend to Aniket's dinner without asking her once why the universe had conspired that we never went out on that private celebratory date I had promised her and had instead found time to visit Aniket's house and who the hell was he to host a party in Mehek's honour by the way? But it did not matter. What mattered was that Mehek's official car was under servicing and so she had asked me to pick her up for the party in my Santro which I was not keen on doing. Her colleagues were the only segment of the universe so far that had not had an opportunity to form their opinions about my recently acquired lifestyle and I would be keen to keep things that way. But she said it had been long since we had spent time with each other and she would rather travel with me in a run-down car than have a taxi driver ferry us to the venue.

'We can park the car a little away from Aniket's house,' she added as an afterthought, an idea I did not mind in the least.

I picked her up from her office at six. We drove on towards Aniket's house in Malabar Hill. Was he also secretly the mayor of the city apart from being an ordinary investment banker, I jokingly asked her but meant to know very seriously how he could afford an apartment in Malabar Hill. She said she had no idea, after which we had very little to talk and so she turned on the radio only to learn that the stereo of the car did not work unless one held its dial between two fingers at all times. So we rolled down the windows and took in the musty evening breeze until we reached a building in Malabar Hill, the boundary wall of which was probably longer than The Great Wall of China.

Aniket resided in all his extravagance in one of the penthouses in the building. By now I was convinced he was involved in some sort of nefarious money-minting activities that Mehek was not privy to. We went up to the top floor and rang the doorbell which played Beethoven's Symphony the number of which I forget. This guy was nuts. He opened the door and ushered us in with a nod. He was dressed in a Tommy Hilfiger polo shirt and cream corduroys from Blackberry's. I shook hands with him as warmly as I could and said customary things about how much I had heard about him etcetera, when he interrupted me and told me that Aniket Sir was inside;

he was his cook. Mehek pulled me away and into the living room which was thronged by Aniket and four more couples who were evidently investment bankers too, because the men had chosen to wear suits inside someone's living room and I was not aware of any other species with such an unbelievable sense of fashion.

A large part of the rest of that evening is a blur, except that I remember feeling severely nauseated by the richness quotient in the room, which was often punctuated by their discussions on how much commission each of them had earned that week via their deals. My gut was so on fire it was auto-combusting whatever I was eating. This also resulted in the slightly embarrassing moment when I got too high on the baked potatoes we had been served and had returned to the table asking for more, only to be told by the cook that the last serving of baked potatoes had been consumed. This was the only time of the evening the other guests had sat up and taken notice of me. After an awkward silence Aniket asked the cook to bake me some more potatoes before allowing the attention of everyone else to return to me.

They learnt from Mehek about my book, which not surprisingly, no one present had heard of. I then mentioned the television show which everybody had heard of and the mention of which made everyone laugh like maniacs. I left them all to continue their group orgasms on the day's stock performance and placed myself before the television with my plate of baked potatoes. I knew Mehek would have her opinion to offer on my behaviour once we returned home. But that was likely to be more bearable than listening to Aniket talk about his latest holiday at some Cambodian resort that I could not afford anyway.

As we prepared to disperse following an arduously long party, Aniket saw us all off at the society gates and asked Mehek where she had parked her car. I told him in not as many words that we had parked our car at safe distance from the view of all the other guests who were preparing to get into their respective cars, each of which looked big enough to accommodate my car in its boot.

'Why did you not park it inside?' demanded Aniket. 'Come, let us all walk you both to your car first.'

I held Aniket firmly by the arm and said that was absolutely unnecessary. But he would have none of it and along with his army of guests, began walking us towards my car which stood atop a sloped road outside his building. Aniket brought out his exaggerated chivalry and said he would not have Mehek walk up the sloped road. He asked me for the keys so he could bring the car to us. Mehek told him indirectly that he was overdoing it now, but he snatched the keys from me. I called out helplessly from behind him and told him that the door on the driver's side would not open and that he would have to get in from the passenger's side. He raised his thumb in acknowledgement even as everyone else looked at each other wide-eyed. I examined Aniket carefully as he walked towards the car: at least six feet two, and a very ample frame. As he crawled into the car from the co-passenger's side, the Santro trembled like a headless chicken.

'Careful,' I shouted. But his upper half was now inside the car, so I could not see his face. I just had to assume he knew what he was doing. Shortly, the Santro started trembling more violently. Aniket's legs, still outside the door, were wriggling like giant cobras. All of us looked at the proceedings, confused, but only until the Santro started looking much larger in size.

'The car is headed downhill. On its own.' One of his super genius banker guests commented.

Yeah, no shit, Sherlock! He could not possibly be reversing that thing downhill with his legs dangling from the other end of the car like helpless twigs. The moron had got some part of his clothing tangled in the hand brake which had now come undone thanks to his weight. It was too late to react. I just moved out of the way and silently watched my poor Santro course its way to doom, just as it had been the first time I had touched it—its silence betraying the physical mutilations it had endured through its life. Against its silence we also heard that buffoon Aniket shrieking for help as his buttocks glided downward against the still air of the night, his head probably dug somewhere in the driver's seat unaware of what was to happen next. And then, quietly, the car went and merged into a curved corner of the other end of the boundary wall.

'Aniket, are you alright?' everyone ran towards the mangled remains of the Santro, least bothered about whatever remained of the poor car. Aniket was brought out after some bit of effort; someone first undid his clothing from the hand brake and then pulled him out of the car, legs first, with his sweaty, horrified face trailing everything else. I was too dazed to react to either of Aniket's state of shock or the devastation that the rear of my car had just suffered. I simply looked at Mehek and gestured that we should leave.

She looked at me as she got into the car, rage and tears stinging her eyes. Yes, of course—absolutely, singularly, my fault that her chivalrous colleague decided to do this little adventure with my car. There was absolutely no more need for an exchange of words between us that night. The writing was on the wall, no pun intended.

23

Big Teachers Don't Cry

MY INTERVIEW WITH Paurush Advani, the owner of Passionate MBA Coaching Centre, lasted under five minutes.

'You are now a part of us until further notice. Congratulations.' He said without a smile. This man never smiled. It was his destiny, as I would learn in some time. I looked at him, confused by the latter half of his sentence. He explained there was nothing to worry; it was a permanent job but only until his business stayed alive—he gestured towards every wall of his office in our sight. Every wall had a story of its own to tell—of betel nut stains, of peeling cement flakes, and of failed MBA aspirations (I concluded this because there were no posters of 'Passionate Student tops CAT with insanely-unbelieveable-percentile'. There was only one motivational poster that read 'Do not be disheartened by failure. It only shows you yet another path that won't take you to success.') Enough said. The betel nut stains and the cement flakes were easy to interpret. Paurush informed me that this building was once jointly owned by a couple—the husband ran a DVD parlour in the left wing and the wife, a beauty parlour in the right wing. The building was sold to Paurush for a song, before he merged both of them to host MBA coaching classes.

The interview gave me a fair idea of what was expected of me while conducting my classes: to try and ensure I did not prematurely quit my job and subject Paurush to further embarrassment. When he had asked me about my expectations from my job, I had told Paurush I was a 'teacher with a difference' and wanted to be able to groom my students into being street smart and ready to be out in the field, slogging it out to prove their worth to the market. At this, he had laughed hysterically, saying those students were smarter than I was presuming them to be, although maybe not in the best sense of the word. And they were ripe enough to be out on the field already, not because they were very intelligent but because they had been attending these coaching classes continuously for the last four years. They had no idea why they wanted to do an MBA. Their parents had forced them into these classes, mainly because IMS, Professional Tutorials, and every other coaching brand that mattered did not accept them. Now Paurush only had room for one batch a year and these worthless students seemed to be in no hurry to leave in order that he could get better students the next time and salvage his reputation.

I looked Paurush firmly in the eye and assured him I would motivate them enough to gun for an admission in an IIM this time round; such was the drive I usually communicated in my leadership speeches. He said he no longer had such high expectations from those students; forget an IIM, he would even be satisfied if I could get some of them an admission in something as third-rate as Excel Institute of Management. I looked at him, tried saying something, then thought better and quietly stood up when he suddenly exclaimed he had completely forgotten to ask me where I had done my MBA from.

'Excel Institute of Management,' I replied with a forced smile.

He said he was delighted to hear that and he was now completely convinced I would be the ideal teacher to those students. He guided me towards a cramped room at the end of the gallery, where he said my students were waiting for me to change their lives forever. He did not say this part with any sort of conviction, for, as he explained in the same breath, these kids had just succeeded in getting their mathematics teacher to quit his job in under two weeks and were now sitting pretty satisfied with themselves.

'Why? What did they do to him?' I asked, my voice trembling.

'He was privy to some bad jokes they made about him,' he shrugged helplessly.

That was not so bad, actually. I could take that. My life had been making a lot of bad jokes about me. That would not be reason enough for me to pick a bone with these students. In fact I could join them in making jokes about me; at least that could help us thaw the ice between us.

'Oh and by the way,' he called out once again. 'I have put up your advertisement on the board. Hopefully some students should give you some leads.'

I closed my eyes and was on my way. The last thing I wanted to think of before walking into a classroom of immature, aimless students was the fact that I was on the verge of homelessness now and needed a place to stay very urgently. After that shameful episode with Aniket and my Santro, I'd had the biggest showdown ever with Mehek. I had tried being reasonable in our arguments, not because I was sensitive or anything, but simply because I was conscious I had walked out on her once before only to return the same night. And my condition had not improved significantly since that episode. I needed the comfort of her water bed even if it came at the cost of some arguments or insults. But then she used the F-word.

'I cannot handle your FINANCES forever!' she screamed.

As any man with dignity must do, I prepared to leave her apartment that very instant. But then I stayed on for an hour in the living room, expecting her to offer an apology. Or say something soothing. Or just say something. Or burp. Nothing happened. I was more scared than I was humiliated. But push had now come to shove. After some bargaining with the owner of the service apartments I had visited earlier, I rented out a room.

I had now been in that room for three days and was left with nearly no money at all. On the second day I had called Mehek, had allowed the phone to ring twice, and had then disconnected the call. When she did not call back, I messaged her saying I had dialled her by mistake and that I hoped she was now warm and happy all by herself in that Goliath of a house. She did not reply. If there was a chance she was waiting to feel sufficiently guilty about the rotten things she had said to me before calling me back, I did not want to lose any more money in the meantime by continuing in that service apartment which, by the way, did not provide any service that justified the premium rent.

I staved off the dirty thoughts of homelessness and strode into the classroom. All students rose and bowed before me in tandem. I obviously knew this was their definition of humour, so I stood before them and bowed back in return before getting straight to the point. I asked them to take out their Word List tutorials without wasting any time in meaningless introductions. Secretly, I was glad none of them recognized me as an author or anything remotely similar. Thus that saved me the hassle of explaining what I was doing in a place like Passionate Coaching Centre, if I was the kind of author my PR agents were trying to project me as. This also meant these wastrels never bothered reading the papers.

'Sir can we take the day off today?' one of them pleaded before I could even get started.

'Why would I let you do that?' I asked without bothering to look up from my copy of the Word List that instantly reminded me of every colleague from the engineering days who had started using these fancy words in the final year of college with sheer desperation, even when they did not make any sense.

'It is too hot, sir,' the student replied.

'Shut up and tell me the meaning of necromancy,' I snarled.

'Sir, if I shut up how will I tell you what it means?'

Everyone laughed. A high standard of humour obviously. I looked at the student. His eyes were red as cherries, his beard dense enough to host a few sparrows, and his smile the kind that suggested it was in the best interest of my prestige to not lock horns with him. Ironically, his name was Vivek. But his qualities totally suggested otherwise.

Alternately, I could try being friendly with them, even if that meant lowering my maturity and intelligence quotient by a few decades or so. Hence, I suggested to them we could have some fun alongside our lessons instead of taking our classes so seriously. They looked as interested as had my audience when I read out sample chapters from my book at all those events.

'I will pick out random words from your Word List,' I instructed them. 'And I will randomly pick one of you, who will promptly form a meaningful sentence using that word.'

'Dude,' Vivek groaned.

'That is so 1993,' someone else said.

I wanted to run straight out of the classroom, through the length of the gallery, and off the balcony of the third floor of this godforsaken building. From a man who everyone believed could conquer the world, I was now a wuss who was not fit enough for any job. I sub-consciously allowed myself to sniffle a little before the class, which became the lowest point of my career. A girl sitting at the front bench noticed my turmoil and quietened the class with a gesture, looked at me with a soft smile and beckoned me to continue what she called 'an exciting game'.

Regaining some lost encouragement, I looked up a word and picked the same girl to form a sentence with it.

'ESCHEW,' I said, asking her to stand up.

She stood up, thought a little, and said, 'My new Verbal Analysis lecturer is so delicious I could chew him.'

'Very funny,' I grunted, but no one heard me because everyone was busy laughing again. The girl looked at me and winked.

'Shut up!' I thundered. A sudden, dark, calm followed. Fear was writ over the students' faces. I felt triumphant. I could have stopped right there. Victory would have been mine. But I proceeded to give them a piece of my mind. And I got too carried away while telling them they needed to start respecting the fact that life was not all about laughter and it got a lot tougher at times and such tough times were capable of making you forget how to giggle like silly teenagers. They listened to me shamefacedly. I could have stopped at that stage. I had conquered them. But then I proceeded to give them my example. I told them about my book, my job, what happened with me at the Lalwani wedding, that the bastard Raghav still owed me money, that I had nowhere to go now, that I missed my Sonata. And I started crying. They were not sniffles any more. I was howling hysterically. And while howling, I realized I now had an additional, a bigger reason to cry: that I had humiliated myself in front of students at least ten years younger than me. I howled louder when this realization dawned upon me.

Presently, a student at the far end of the classroom started crying in harmony with me. I stopped and looked sharply at him. The tears looked genuine. The girl sitting next to him told me he got carried away by emotions too easily. But I could not trust these cheapskates any more. I just picked up my bag and walked out of the classroom, wondering if never coming back was a plausible option. Could I try what my maids did so often, so adeptly? Could I tell Paurush I needed some advance salary, collect it, and then never come back? Shit.

24

Fall From Grace

MY APPOINTMENT WITH Shivang Apte at the Taj was four days after having used that utterly useless bar of soap provided by the management at the serviced apartment—the kind of junk that does not generate any foam, leave alone any kind of smell. And because I had firmly resolved to minimize expenditures on groceries, I had been judiciously using this soap for my shower. And it also doubled up as my shaving foam or whatever became of it when I applied it to my cheeks.

Shivang insisted I attend his book reading event at the banquet hall before we caught up for coffee.

I wanted to say, 'I smell like a skunk, and I look like the "before" part of a *Khushhaali Yantra* advertisement on Teleshopping. And I have enough reasons to be crabby, so I don't need to see you steal the limelight from under my nose as I sit in the audience wondering how much a trip back home in a taxi might cost me.' But I just said that I would have loved to come, but was wary of the media. And I was not big on interviews that day as I needed some mental space to focus on research for my next book. Suitably impressed, he agreed to see me at the coffee shop after his event. I was made to wait half an hour before he joined me, apologetic when he did not need to be.

'Escaping the shutterbugs is not easy,' I said, forcing myself to smile.

Just then a girl sprang up from her seat at an adjacent table and surprised Shivang with an awkward hug. She identified herself as his 'biggest fan', took a selfie with him without his permission, and then ran back to her table gleefully. I wanted to leave already.

'How do you handle the attention?' I asked.

'It is hard earned,' he said. 'I just try to respect it every way I can.'

He even bloody *spoke* like a celebrity. Yaar he was not *so* great also, come on!

He ordered a *Death By Chocolate*, the name of which was very apt because it cost eight hundred rupees. I just ordered a single espresso shot which would cost me one dinner—just in case Shivang did not offer to pay. We chatted endlessly, but only until we arrived at the subject of our books' sales, after which I allowed him to do all the talking.

'Do you know the first time someone emailed me with feedback on my book?' His eyes bored into the still air contemplatively as he made room for the steward to place the *Death by Chocolate* before him. I had now lost interest in what Shivang was saying. I wanted to eat that thing. He could have my espresso shot. I was once spoilt for choices. I was now stripped of them.

The espresso tasted like crap. As expected. I finished it in one gulp and then looked at Shivang again.

'So, you were saying?' I drew his attention again.

He happily took a large gulp of the chocolate mound and commented on what a delicacy I was missing out on. I wanted to shove his head inside that bowl. That would be some death by chocolate, if you please.

'I was saying the first feedback email on my book was written to me almost two months after the book was published,' he said. 'Do you know why?'

'Of course,' I replied. 'Those jerk store owners must not have stocked your book on display. I have been through the drill.'

'No, the book was always there,' he replied. 'But no one had noticed it.'

Clearly he had done something revolutionary to rectify this, something that had not occurred to me yet. Because clearly, his book was now getting all the attention he could have asked for.

'I picked one bookstore per week and stood outside it four hours a day,' he explained, the beginning of which did not sound exciting at all. 'And I stopped every customer at the entrance and showed him my book, urging him to pick it up.'

'And what did the customers think of it?' I asked doubtfully.

'Varied responses,' he laughed. 'But mostly I got a lot of spite.'

So basically, he had turned into a heckler? That was desperate enough. Did I subscribe to such tactics? Not at all. But were such tactics the need of the hour? That depended on how well they worked for Mr Apte.

'Of course they worked,' he said. 'Every four out of ten customers smiled at me and said they would definitely pick up my book. Every three of those four actually made it a point to pick it up from the shelf and cast a glance. One of those three would buy it as well.'

'A 10 per cent success rate,' I pondered. 'Some solace, eh?'

'A matter of pride and achievement, actually,' he said. 'Baby steps propel a giant leap.'

'And now that you have made the giant leap, no one will care what the baby steps were,' I smiled.

'But I will. Forever,' he said.

The bill was brought to our table. I was just about to fake having received a phone call so that I could disappear from the scene and re-emerge after the bill had been cleared. But Shivang saved me the trouble by slipping in his platinum credit card and handing it back to the steward. Shit. I used to have that card once, before it got cancelled for a non-payment of four hundred rupees.

'Someone had asked me how I handle my success,' he continued. 'The answer is very simple. I lap it up hungrily on schedule—because I fell from grace far too many times before acquiring this success. It has come at a great price.'

Of course. This was it, wasn't it? The inevitable fall from grace. That need to get off my high horse and realize I was no longer the dominant, suave player I once was. Moreover, falling from grace was hardly a challenge after my emotional outburst before those shameless students in the classroom the other day. How much more could I fear falling from grace? There was so much more scope to fall lower and get some traction on the book again. I knew what I had to do.

I ran back to the serviced apartment and connected to the unprotected wi-fi the guy in the adjacent room had been using (some goodness still existed in the world). The plan was simple. I would do a Paulo Coelho on the entire city. I would bulk order my own book from an online vendor and then ring every doorbell in Mumbai and start selling it at a discount. YES! I WOULD FALL FROM GRACE AND RISE. To my part-dismay and part-excitement, the book was sold out on at least three online stores. I was extremely surprised because as far as I knew, my parents were the only ones who had been buying copies of my book of late and had been gifting it at every party they had been attending. This could not have accounted for the book going out of stock.

I called the customer helpline of one of the vendors to make enquiries. The guy was not very helpful; he said the book was very obviously out of stock which very obviously meant he had no copies and no information to provide to me. I probed him for details: was the book out of stock because it had sold an insane number of copies or because the vendors had stopped procuring it altogether. He could not confirm for sure, but then he added that given he had never heard of this book himself it was more likely that the vendor had not been bothering to procure it at all. Later in the conversation he realized he was speaking to the author and changed tack, saying he was pretty sure it had been selling like hot cakes.

So much for customer support. I turned off the laptop and put myself to sleep. I would need to mull over my options the next morning.

Sometime in the thick of night, I received a phone call.

'Sir, this is Vivek from Passionate Coaching Classes,' said the voice.

'Huh?'

'Sir, the guy who made fun of you in class the other day?'

'Brilliant,' I grunted. 'Now what do you want from me?'

'Sir, you need a place to stay, don't you?'

'Yes. And?'

'I am coming to pick you up in ten minutes, Sir,' he said hurriedly. 'Please be ready.'

Fifteen minutes later Vivek was helping me load my bags into my car.

'Does it run?' He asked, looking at the rear of the Santro.

'No, but it crawls beautifully,' I replied as we drove off.

I was still unsure what he had in mind. I drove us to his hostel in Juhu.

'You have to be kidding me, man,' I said.

'Sir, it is free of cost,' he said excitedly. 'No one will find out.'

'You are sneaking me in?'

He handed me the identity card of some student who had graduated from their college in 2004. He said every impostor had been using the same identity card for the last ten years and it had all been going perfectly. I just needed to flash it before the guard's eyes confidently and then stroll in through the gates. I followed his instructions. He took me up to a room that was exactly as big as the main bathroom in Mehek's apartment. God, I missed her even more now. Four bed rolls were thrown carelessly on the floor. Cigarette butts lay strewn all around. Three toothbrushes stood in an empty bottle of Old Monk on the floor right outside a bathroom the door of which did not close entirely and which had a gaping hole at its bottom. Two students with thin goatees lay slouched on the bed rolls, smiling at me as though they had been instructed in advance by Vivek.

'What is the catch?' I looked at all of them suspiciously. 'Why are you being so nice?'

'I feel repentant, Sir,' Vivek said, and then the other two boys burst into giggles.

'Ok, maybe I should just go back,' I pretended to leave, but he held me back.

'Alright, Sir, I will tell you,' he began. 'Let us just say this is a symbiotic arrangement.'

He made me sit on the only table present in the room—there were no chairs. (Three weeks later I discovered there was one chair, in fact, but I had never noticed it because there were, at any given time, at least thirty dirty clothes lying on top of it in an ugly mound). He handed me some print outs that looked like questionnaires.

'Ah, a market research project?' I looked at him and smiled.

He sheepishly explained he had been thinking all along that Market Research was an optional subject he had applied for in the final year of his BBA course. And he had discovered only the previous night that the optional subject was Brand Building, which he had been studying diligently all along. And Market Research, in fact, was a mandatory subject that he was most likely to flunk because he had to interview over two hundred consumers on their soap-buying habits before preparing some detailed analytical report to support his findings.

'Alright, consider your work done,' I said, taking the printouts in my hand.

Vivek shook my hand violently. 'Thank you, Sir! I do not know how I can begin thanking you!'

'Behaving yourself in the coaching class tomorrow will be a good start,' I replied.

25

The Resurgence

Dear Nakul,

It gives us immense pleasure to invite you to our annual conclave this September. Your book 'The Chaos Project' has become a cult sensation in our organization and has given our employees a profound insight into what kind of employee one should not be. Should you be able to spare your valuable time, we would like you to take an hour's session with our employees and give them a motivational talk on corporate competitiveness and scruples. Kindly let us know if you will be interested, and we will send you the event details subsequently.

Regards,
The Human Resources Department (HRD),
Pragmatic Solutions Inc.

Dear HRD,

I am happy to know I have been of help to your employees. I will check my schedule and respond to you. Meanwhile please provide me details on the remuneration you will be providing me.

Regards,
Nakul Kapoor

Dear Nakul,

Our sincerest apologies, our conclave does not account for remuneration to speakers unless they are known public figures. We regret that we will not be able to accommodate you at the conclave if you were seeking remuneration.

Regards,
The HRD,
Pragmatic Solutions Inc.

Dear HRD,

That's absolutely alright! As you would know I am a self-sufficient person who dwells in his world of creativity, which does not have room for trivialities like commercial gains. I sought remuneration only to ensure I maintain a consistent market rate, lest tomorrow various other organizations start expecting me to conduct such sessions with them for free. Given we are talking about an organization as reputed as yours, I am willing to make an exception and speak to your employees free of cost. Please send me the event details, I will look forward to coming.

Regards,
Nakul

The big question, of course, was what was wrong with the employees of this company? What part of my near-extinct book had so caught their fancy that they had accorded it a cult status? Unless, wait. This could have been another prank by my students. I had never heard of a company called Pragmatic Solutions. I looked up Google. Ok, there did exist such a company. I saw their emails once again. The signature at the email seemed to have a legitimate phone number that belonged to the company's board. Nothing seemed fishy. I paced around the hostel room in anticipation of their response. I was not so excited about going to speak about my book before some few hundred employees as I was to see the faces of those people who had so fallen in love with my work. Restless, I began cleaning the room, God knows why. I felt like my roommates' nanny—sweeping away their burnt ciggies, folding their clothes, and making the room look like a room while they were away in college making merry.

It had now been three hours since I last wrote to Pragmatic Solutions. They had not replied yet. Were they still upset I had asked for remuneration, those touchy people?

Dear HRD,

Awaiting your response to my last email. If you would like to invite me to your conclave please do so promptly so that I do not commit to any of the numerous other institutions that have been chasing me to schedule time with them.

Regards,
Nakul Kapoor

Dear Nakul,

We are happy to note that you have flexed your commercial preferences as well as your tight schedule strictly for us; sure, we confirm extending an invite to you via this email. A contact from our team will get in touch with you soon on the exact date and time slot.
Thanks.

The HRD,
Pragmatic Solutions

What the fuck was that winkie for? HR would remain the same wherever they went. Oversmart and underworked.

Anyway, this was a happy moment! Some people in some corner of the world had appreciated my work. I did a little cartwheel and then went about exploring the exclusive inbox I had once reserved only for fan mails but which I had stopped checking long ago on seeing the futility of the entire exercise. To my pleasant surprise, this mailbox was ticking too! Readers had written in from various cities, saying (mostly) how much they had loved the book. What I failed to understand was how so many people had mysteriously gone missing from the face of the earth when I was nose-diving into the debris of my ego all those months. Well, the respite was welcome at whatever stage it had come. I spent time replying personally to each email—one, because I had a lot of time to kill those days; two, because reaching out to these people in response was my only hope of continuing this online propagation. The only emails I did not respond to were from those who sought help to get published themselves.

YEAH LIKE THERE IS NOT ENOUGH COMPETITION IN THE MARKET TO WRECK MY LIFE ALREADY!

Actually, there was another email I did not respond to, for the first few days. A girl had read my book and had been writing to me twice a day, expecting a reply. But the question she had been asking me in every email was the kind that could have excited me, say, twelve years ago. Now it only disturbed me a little: 'Are you single?' Given there was no polite way to respond to this question, I chose not to respond at all. But she would not take no response for an answer, so ultimately I responded that it was best if we caught up sometime like good friends do over coffee so that I could get to know her better before answering such personal and sensitive questions.

Meanwhile the book had picked up steam in segments other than corporate houses too. Paurush got to know of the book from one of his friends and instantly changed the promotional campaign of Passionate Coaching Centre to '…with Verbal Analysis tutored by none other than reputed novelist Nakul Kapoor.' I had been in some discussions with him to do the right thing by sharing some profits with me in return for using my name in bolstering his business. He did not agree because that far my name had not helped bolster his business in the first place. At least the students had some respect for me now, or so they pretended to show in class. We were all back in the classroom and I was still the butt of the occasional joke. But the bright side was we had all agreed to practice our reading and comprehension sessions using my book, so it was a win-win situation.

I had nearly finished helping Vivek with his extremely boring Market Research project. We were interviewing the last leg of consumers outside a mall when a teenager came up to me and asked me if I was Nakul Kapoor. When I nodded, he showed me a copy of my book he had just bought from a store inside.

'It had better be good,' he said before walking off.

Vivek accompanied me as I went into the bookstore. Twelve copies of the book were present. As was always the case, the store manager did not seem to know where in the store they were placed. We spotted them an hour later, individual copies hidden in various corners of the maze of books, like the Da Vinci code.

'But it is doing very well, I can assure you,' said the manager when he learnt he was talking to the writer.

'All of you say the same thing,' I said sourly.

'I am serious,' he said, showing me the back cover. 'Look, ever since your publisher slashed the price of the book, things took a turn for the better. Customers got more receptive.'

I called Swarup, who continued to insist he was only playing by conservative business rules of supply and demand. He said there was a surge in the online purchase of the book last month which prompted vendors to order larger quantities from him. He (finally) saw sense in reducing the price of the book, and the vendors in turn were willing to give better discounts to their customers. He said he did not know the trigger, because he had given up hope on my book way before I did. But he was happy with the outcome nonetheless.

Vivek was ecstatic. 'Why don't you promote your book in our college?'

'I can think about it,' I said. 'What will your college pay me?'

'In fact, you might have to pay the college,' he said. 'I was thinking of a book stall you could set up at our college fun fair...'

'Please!' I said, stomping off as he tried to keep pace with me. 'Maintain some class before me, boss!'

~

The mysterious girl responded in a couple of days. 'Gloria's Coffee, Bandra?'

I agreed. Now I would not have you misconstrue the situation, but only because the poor girl was investing so much faith and energy in meeting me in person, I decided to go for a general hygiene and appearance upheaval that was in order for many months already. I spent the first half of the day getting a facial makeover at a nearby spa, before heading over to Gloria's Coffee. I was tempted to order a Crunchy Nut Frappe, but that would not register well with the image of a serious writer. So I ordered a cup of espresso and waited patiently, pondering the endless possibilities if by any remote chance I connected mentally and emotionally with this girl and also if other unimportant trivialities, such as good looks, were in place.

'Autograph, please!' Hearing her voice, my gaze first fell on the outstretched hand that held my book.

Horror of horrors! How on earth had I allowed this to happen to me? Once again, Mehek had scored a mental victory over me. This girl would never cease to show how well she knew me.

'So you were ready to make the scene already with someone else?' She asked, taking off her business blazer. Thank God for small mercies.

'Not that I care, but you have gotten a little hotter since I last saw you,' I said, trying hard not to look into her eyes.

'It does look like you care,' she said. 'And you bloody well must. I thought you would have had the sense to figure out by now that it takes two to tango.' She pointed at my book.

'Are you trying to tell me you are the generator of this sudden wave I am riding on?' I asked in disbelief.

All it took was a little bit of common sense, she said. She had ordered twenty copies more than a month ago from an online vendor. For the bulk order, she had won a 30 per cent discount on the purchase. She resold the copies to twenty of her colleagues who had interests other than fantasizing about the Bombay Stock Exchange. These twenty colleagues followed her lead, bulk-ordered copies at discounts, and sold them to their friends in return at the original market price. They had hence— read my book, recommended and sold it ahead, and had made fat profits themselves. Totally expected from investment bankers.

'The trick of the trade was passed on at every layer,' she smiled. 'You will be surprised what we can all be made to do for a little bit of extra money.'

I fetched us two cups of Cappuccino. I paid. I had never felt as comfortable paying for a bland cup of coffee in the past year.

'Ask me about it,' I said, handing her one cup. 'A little bit of extra money is all I have thought of in the year gone by.'

'Come home,' she held my hand and clenched it.

At this point it was appropriate to go all emotional or

all romantic on her, but the only emotion I could feel was of jubilation. Of course I tried not to project it blatantly, but I alone knew how I had survived close to fifty days in that hostel room with Vivek, his doped-out friends, and Rakesh the Rodent, who had an appointment in the bathroom every morning before I could make it. They were nice boys, but they had messed up the wiring in my head. My lowest point was when I got drunk with them in their room and we all tried offering some Old Monk to Rakesh too. He had gratefully accepted our offer. But then we had to spend the next morning mopping up rat urine spotted at various corners of the room.

'I should have been more patient with you,' Mehek continued. 'I should not have panicked. But I just could not see where your ambitions were leading both of us to.'

It took her fifty days to admit her fault! Did she know how much I had panicked in those fifty days after I had left the comfort of her water bed?

'Unsettling you has surely done you some good too,' she comforted me. 'You will be a wiser man now.'

'Thanks for the compliment,' I replied. 'Now I am really hungry. When do we go home?'

26

The End of the Beginning

My publicists telephone me early one morning and ask me to pick up the newspaper immediately. Since it has been over four weeks since they last spoke to me, I assume they are excited for a very good reason. I struggle out of bed, Mehek tailing me sleepily. I pick up the newspaper lying at the door and skim through the pages. And then I am totally woken up by what I read on page 8:

Novelist Nakul Kapoor terms chick-lit literature 'a waste of time'

In a conversation with Nakul Kapoor about his favourite writers and about the changing face of Indian literature today, the author told us, tongue-in-cheek, that he was appalled by the sudden rise in the number of women who have gotten into the habit of writing 'sketchy feminist stories led by protagonists with some vague sense of sexual liberation'. He said he was numbed by a few such books he had begun to read and had surmised early in the day that they would be a 'complete waste of time'.

Kapoor's outburst has sparked off an outrage on Twitter since last night, led mainly by chick-lit writers who feel they have been personally targeted by his insensitive and irreverent remarks that reek of insecurity and misogyny. Even as the hashtag #YoNakulKapoorSoCheap trends on the social networking site, we have been unable to establish contact with the man in question himself. We wonder if he will be as good with his words in his forthcoming books as he is with his so-called repartees that he has not justified as yet.

I call the publicists back and demand to know exactly what is going on. As far as I can remember, I had met a correspondent at their behest the previous evening and had only said 'I do not read chick-lit literature so I do not have an opinion on it' when I was asked to say something on the subject.

'That is the idea!' say the publicists in delight. They colluded with the correspondent the previous night and 'just tweaked my statement a little'.

'A little?' I ask in disbelief. 'What are we going to do about all the hate?'

'We do nothing about it,' they say. 'The hate will spike up the sales even more. Trust us.'

I am not so sure I must trust them. You see, I am no longer the guy who needed cheap gimmicks to stay alive in the market. Yes, it was justifiable three months ago, when my book had only begun to resurface in the market thanks to some concerted multilevel marketing efforts spurred by Mehek. At that time, I *desired* cheap publicity stunts and my publicists gave me none. And now they have put me in this soup. I am not happy. I now command a certain respect from my audience. I am someone whose words are taken seriously by everyone barring a few people like Mehek, my mother, and my car cleaner. I seriously do not need this chaos now.

I log into Twitter. The timeline has gone bonkers abusing me. Ladies are spewing hate. Men who will do anything to show they are not misogynists are spewing hate too. And clueless teenagers who do not know what #YoNakulKapoorSoCheap is all about are making the lamest jokes using this hashtag anyway. Mehek thinks this is good news because now a lot more people will buy my book even if it is out of pure hate. How do I explain to her the sales are now almost a secondary priority? I have an image that is more at stake here. The latest edition of *Jansatta* has bolstered me to the twenty-second spot in the list of rising youth in Indian literature. I am now increasingly conscious of my social responsibilities alongside my business interests.

I try posting a tweet clarifying I have been misunderstood. But I only get more hate in return. The publicists suggest that if I am willing to pay them a premium, they can organize a group to burn my effigy next to Flora Fountain and that can be shown live on at least two news channels. Thanks, but no thanks, I politely decline.

Later that evening, Vivek comforts me with the news that together with his friends, he has managed to create fifty-three fake identities on Twitter who are sending a lot of counter-hate back to all my haters. A new hashtag #ProudofyouNakulKapoor has begun trending and is catching up with the earlier one steadily. I am proud of Vivek. Not only did he pass his final exams with minimal scares, he and the other useless students in that coaching class have finally got off Paurush's back and have left the coaching centre. A few of them have actually even managed to get an MBA somewhere. Vivek has not. Instead, he has now been made to join his father's business of chemical dyes. Only, he does not go to his father's office either. He says he will, someday.

That's alright. Everyone finds his calling sooner or later, yes? I found mine, then lost it for a lot of time, and then regained it. I am still not the male JK Rowling or even a tenth of her, but I am at least Nakul Kapoor. I never got, and I no longer want, that fraud contract from that swine Brian. I have not yet forgiven myself for all the money I wasted on his fraudulent schemes for nothing. But I am beginning to reconcile slowly. If following my dream would require me to walk on a smooth road, there would be no romance in the pursuit of the dream. And then all those (sometimes misleading) inspirational movies about following your dream despite all obstacles, would be rendered meaningless. I continue spending money on promoting my book now, much to the delight of my publicists who keep egging me on. This also makes my publisher happy, and I have just learnt from him that the book has gone into the fourth print run and is doing decent business. I have sent him a polite reminder about the royalty cheque he was to send me last month. I am awaiting his reply.

Speaking of money, guess what I received last week? A cheque from Raghav. I would not have been further baffled had he not topped it up with a note that said 'Hey sorry I could not return your money in time, I was away on holiday.' Why had he even bothered with this explanation? I obviously knew he was away on a holiday for the last two years and more; of course I understood he needed the leeway.

I accepted the cheque, but not his idiotic explanation.

Mehek and I are finally getting married this year. I am still not looking for a job. Her parents have stopped expecting me to look for one. But whenever a relative meets us, they never fail to clarify that I had abandoned my earlier job by choice and not by force. Our parents like each other, and that is a big relief. They are only arguing over the venue of the wedding. Mehek and I have comfortably steered ourselves out of this conversation. We have just returned from a nice holiday in Koh Samui, which none of us had to pay for. She won the best employee or something, for which Goldman Sachs had sent her, and when I threw some fits about it she tried reasoning with the management to sponsor her fiancé's ticket, which they magically agreed to.

At night before we hit the sack, I log in to check the status on Twitter. The drama there has finally ceased to my relief. But just then, I notice, a new one is waiting to begin. I have an email from Bytesphere's HR, which, to no real surprise, has failed to recognize they are writing to an ex-employee. The email says that a lot of their employees have read my book and are keen that I hold an interactive session with them on *The Joie De Vivre of Integrated Team Management* because this spirit is in keeping with their core values of transparency, mutual respect for employees and commitment towards a positive working atmosphere.

This is the most entertaining mail I have read in the longest time I can remember. A big grin flashes across my face as I reply: 'Let me check my calendar.'